A CALL FOR NURSE TEMPLAR

Young Mrs. Craig, one of Linden's midwifery
patients, seemed to be firmly under the thumb
of her husband's brother, the arrogant Randal
Craig. When Linden found out Randal's
opinion of *her*, it was the last straw!

A CALL FOR NURSE TEMPLAR

BY

ANNE WEALE

MILLS & BOON LIMITED
London . Sydney . Toronto

First published in Great Britain 1960 by Mills &
Boon Limited, 17-19 Foley Street, London W1A 1DR

This edition 1978
© Anne Weale 1960
Australian copyright 1978
Philippine copyright 1978

ISBN 0 263 72850 1

Set in 10 on 11pt. Baskerville

Made and printed in Great Britain by
C. Nicholls & Company Ltd
The Philips Park Press, Manchester

To
SYLVIA VAUGHAN, C.S.M.,
with my warmest thanks for her help
with the book and the baby.

CHAPTER ONE

"I've found you a corner seat and stowed your cases on the rack. There's only some elderly chap in the compartment, and he's buried in paper work, so you should be able to catch up on your sleep."

Linden turned from the station bookstall where she had been choosing magazines for her journey and smiled her thanks at Rupert Ellis.

Although she had had only a few hours' rest between the end of the Forresters' dance and a scrambled seven o'clock breakfast, she did not look tired. She was used to late nights and, at twenty-four, had not yet lost the abundant vitality of healthy youth.

"Oh, bless you, Rupert — but I wish you hadn't dragged out of bed to see me off. I could have managed quite well with a taxi."

"That's your trouble — you're much too independent," he answered wryly. "I wish you weren't going such a devil of a way. Can't you change your mind and stay in London?"

"Certainly not! I'm looking forward to it," she said, laughing at him. "Anyway, it's only two hours by train. You can easily come to see me if you want to."

He moved closer, taking her free hand in his. "You know I do, Linden," he said, in a low tone. "But if I come you're sure to be tied up most of the time."

"Not all the time," Linden said cheerfully, hoping that he was not going to choose this moment of departure for some emotional declaration. It had not been until the previous evening that she had begun to suspect that he was getting rather too serious about her. They had known each other so long – since their schooldays, in fact – that she looked on him almost as a brother.

"It's nearly time to leave. I'd better get settled," she said quickly. "Thank you for taking me about so much, Rupert. As soon as I get my bearings, I'll write you a long screed."

"The train won't leave for a minute. Look, Linden . . ."

But Linden had already extricated her hand and was moving towards the express. If Rupert did imagine himself in love with her – and it was probably only a passing infatuation, because they had spent so much time together recently – it would only make matters worse to let him declare himself.

"Don't wait any longer. I'm sure you're longing to get back to bed," she said over her shoulder, as they walked down the corridor to her compartment.

"I could come up next weekend if you're off duty," he said hopefully.

"Oh, I doubt if I will be, Rupert – and anyway I shall be busy getting my flat straight."

"I could give you a hand."

"No, I don't think so. I really must concentrate on work for a week or two."

As they reached the compartment he had found for her, she turned and held out her hand. "Thanks again for the fun – and don't break your neck in that souped-up juggernaut while I'm away."

A porter passed down the platform, slamming doors, and a whistle blew. Further along the corridor people were leaning out of windows to call last-moment messages.

"Oh, do go, Rupert, or you may get stuck," Linden said hurriedly. She was always fidgety when people stayed on the trains until the very last second, and particularly so in this instance.

"You promise to write?" Rupert said urgently.

8

"Yes, of course – but do *go*!" she exclaimed.

"All right. Goodbye. Take care of yourself." His grip on her hand was painfully tight.

And then, as the train began to shudder and Linden tried to free her hand and push him to the door, he gave a kind of stifled groan and drew her into his arms. She was still gasping from the impact of his kiss when he leapt from the now moving train and began to run alongside, calling something unintelligible through the window to her.

It was not until the train passed the end of the platform and Rupert was forced to give up mouthing and gesticulating that Linden recovered her breath. His kiss, though necessarily brief, had confirmed her worst fears. Indeed the very fact that he had kissed her at all in public showed the strength of his new emotions, because in most respects he was a fairly conventional young man. That he should kiss her in public *and* with so much ardour was really alarming. He must have been holding himself in check for much longer than she had realized or he would never have given way to such a demonstration.

"Oh, dear, why on earth didn't I sense it earlier?" she thought worriedly. "Now we shall have to have a showdown, and it will spoil everything."

By this time the train was under full steam and, straightening her floppy straw hat with its bright scarf knotted round the crown, which Rupert's embrace had knocked askew, Linden turned to enter the compartment. As she closed the door behind her, one of her magazines slipped to the floor and her travelling companion bent to retrieve it for her.

"Oh . . . thank you." Still preoccupied with Rupert, Linden gave him an absent-minded smile. Then, as their eyes met, a rush of embarrassed colour suffused her cheeks and she almost snatched the magazine from his hand.

It showed Rupert's condition that he should have described him as "some elderly chap", she thought vexedly. He was actually quite a young man, probably in his early thirties. But what was really infuriating and the cause of her violent blush was that, however deep in papers he might have been earlier on, he had obviously seen the incident in the corridor. In fact, judging from the quizzical gleam in his keen dark eyes, he had barefacedly watched the whole thing and derived considerable amusement from it.

Suddenly aware that her lipstick was probably smudged, Linden slammed down her belongings and hurriedly opened a magazine. She would have liked to light a cigarette and recover herself slowly, but she could feel that the man was still watching her and was afraid that her hands would start trembling.

The sing-song voice of a steward announcing breakfast offered an escape, and as soon as he reached their compartment Linden jumped up again and was directed to the restaurant car. But she had scarely had time to glance at the menu when her fellow traveller appeared in the doorway and, much to her fury, the head waiter led him to her table.

"Damn him! I believe he's followed me on purpose," she thought angrily.

However, when he gave his order without glancing at her and opened a morning paper, her normal good sense reasserted itself. No doubt he had watched Rupert's impassioned farewell and been amused by it, but she would probably have been guilty herself in similar circumstances. It was Rupert who was really to blame for her embarrassment.

By the time she had eaten some cornflakes and had a cup of coffee – her first breakfast had consisted of a single slice of toast – Linden had quite recovered. Even her concern for Rupert was giving place to excited anticipation of the new job ahead of her.

The dining car was now almost full up, and when two tall American tourists arrived, they were shown to Linden's table.

At first, eating her bacon and eggs with the healthy appetite that never affected her slim supple figure, Linden paid little attention to the new arrivals. When one of them, catching her eye, remarked that it looked like being a hot day, she agreed pleasantly that it did. It was not until an exchange of commonplaces had begun to develop into a definite conversation that she realised that the man from her compartment was watching her again, and with an unmistakable glint of mockery.

Linden had two elder brothers, each with a host of friends. Even in her teens she had been natural and at ease in masculine company, and it was not her habit to be shy or wary of strangers in normal circumstances. She had answered the young American out of common politeness, but the possibility that this annoying man opposite thought she was encouraging a "pick-up" put a rapid brake on her friendliness. As soon as she had finished her toast, she asked for the bill, paid it, and returned to the compartment.

She had a twenty-minute respite before the dark man rejoined her. Linden ignored his entry, and when he asked permission to smoke, assented coldly without even looking at him.

A few minutes later the door slid open again and the American appeared.

"Say, ma'am, I hope I didn't offend you ... talking to you back there," he said awkwardly.

"Why – of course not," Linden said, rather startled.

He shifted uncertainly. "Well ... you left kind of quickly, so I just wanted to be sure." He paused, obviously waiting for a lead. None came, so after some further hesitation he said, "Well ... that's okay, then,

I guess. That's fine. It's surely been a pleasure to have met you, ma'am."

Feeling rather a beast, Linden smiled and watched him leave. She gathered that he had only recently arrived in England, and she hoped the episode wouldn't make him think that all English people were friendly one moment and markedly offhand the next.

For some moments after he had gone, there was silence. Then the man in the opposite corner said quietly, "It must be that stunning hat you're wearing."

Linden gave him a cool stare, her eyebrows lifted.

"I was suggesting that your very becoming hat might partly account for all this pursuit," he said, smiling.

If he had been almost anyone else, she would probably have coloured a little and laughed and thought no more of it. But something in his manner nettled her, and instead she gave him a freezing look and said, "I'm afraid I don't follow you. Excuse me."

In the rather unattractive sanctuary of the washroom, she lit a cigarette and contemplated the grubby handbasin with professional disapproval. Perhaps it was lack of sleep that made her so edgy; that, and a certain trepidation about how she would fit into her new surroundings.

Glancing at her watch, she saw that they were already more than halfway to her destination. She took off her hat and began to comb her silky fair hair. When she was working, she pinned it into a smooth swathe at the back of her head, partly because it was tidier and partly it made her look older and more authoritative. But this morning, in a rush to catch the train, she had left it loose, the ends curling gently inwards to her slender neck, one thick soft lock slanting carelessly across her forehead.

In striking contrast to her hair, her brows and lashes were dark, although, unlike her sister Louise, she had not the additional distinction of brilliant gentian blue eyes. Linden's eyes were grey and the bridge of her short straight nose was lightly scattered with freckles which, in her teens, she had used every means to eradicate. Now she accepted them with humorous resignation, just as she accepted what her father called "that pugnacious chin". She would never be a beauty like Louise, but at least she had a reasonable figure and satisfactory legs.

Having repaired her light make-up, she made her way slowly back along the corridor. The train was pulling into a station and she was relieved when a woman with two children came into the compartment – although she was less grateful for their company when both youngsters started to bawl in ear-splitting concert. Ten minutes of sustained howling drove the dark man into the corridor, and Linden, although equally deafened, gained a certain malicious satisfaction from his disrupted comfort.

Watching him as he leaned an arm against the window rail, his other hand thrust into his trouser pocket, she thought he was the type that appealed to Louise. In this, as in most other respects, the sisters differed. Louise liked escorts to be urbane and worldly with a challenging element of arrogance. She derided the big, boisterous, hard-up young men whom the younger girl seemed to attract, calling them "Linden's Great Danes" and mocking their lack of polish.

The man half turned to watch some feature of the fleeting landscape, and Linden studied his profile, noting strongly marked brows and the forceful cut of his jaw. It was a proud face, she decided, with more than a suggestion of severity when the mouth was in repose and one could not see his eyes. He took out his cigarette case and, noticing his lean flexible hands and short, scrubbed nails, Linden wondered if he could possibly be a doctor.

No, of course not, she told herself firmly to quiet that

faint prick of alarm. No provincial G.P. wore an immaculate grey suit, and he was almost certainly too young to be a consultant. Anyway, he might not be getting off at the same stop. Even if he were, the town to which she was going was not so small that there was any risk of another encounter.

As the train chugged slowly through the sidings, Linden looked with interest at the entrance to her new home. After the vast cavernous gloom of Liverpool Street, this station had almost an intimate atmosphere. The houses above the cuttings were cleaner and better kept than the bleak sooty tenements of Bethnal Green and Stratford, and the clothes lines flapped briskly in the breeze instead of hanging like limp grey shrouds above squalid back yards where sunlight never penetrated.

Linden rose to lift down her cases, but as she stretched up to the rack, two grey-sleeved arms reached over her head and the man said, "Let me do that for you."

He swung them down to the seat with muscular ease, acknowledging her thanks with the slightest quirk of his lips. For the first time in her life Linden found herself resenting the physical superiority of the male. It must have been men like this, whose whole manner suggested a kind of tolerant patronage for everything feminine, that had sparked the suffragette movement, she thought impatiently.

Fortunately there was a porter nearby when the train drew to a halt, so she was saved from having to accept his assistance to the barrier. Indeed, by the time her cases had been put on a trolley, the man had disappeared in the stream of passengers hurrying towards the ticket lodge.

The few station taxis had all been taken when they reached the parking yard, and Linden left the porter to guard her luggage and went to wash. She did not want to present herself to the Non-Medical Superintendent at the Clinic with travel-grubby hands and a shiny nose.

Through the open window of the cloakroom she could hear the muted rumble of buses passing the station gates and the distant clangour of a fire engine or ambulance. The sensation of beginning a whole new phase of her life sent a faint tremor of excitement through her. Dimly, her mind on the opportunities and friendships that lay ahead, Linden heard the click of high heels and a woman's voice, husky and faintly drawling, apologising for keeping someone waiting. But it was the reply that arrested her attention, for the man's voice was all too familiar – it was that of her disliked *vis-à-vis* in the train.

"This is a very pleasant surprise, Melanie – but where's Andrew?" she heard him ask.

"Oh, he was busy so I offered to come in his place," the woman replied carelessly. Then, in a provocative tone: "Don't you like my sun tan, or haven't you even noticed it?"

"Yes, of course; you look very fit. Did you have a good holiday?"

"Oh, the usual thing – nothing exciting happened," the woman replied in a bored tone. Linden heard a low, caressing laugh before she added, "Really, Randal, you are *quite* the most ungallant man I know. Here I am, browned to perfection and wearing my prettiest dress for you, and all you can say is that I look fit. A very lukewarm reception, I must say."

"What did you want me to tell you?" the man asked, with a laugh. "That you look like a Tahitian goddess?"

"Do I?" the woman asked softly, and Linden could imagine the seductive upward glance that accompanied the question.

The man called Randal laughed again. "What a vain little minx you are, Melanie. Where's the car? I could do with a wash and some coffee."

"It won't be long. We got here early, so I sent Rogers

to fetch a parcel for me. He should be back by now. Poor you, having to come home by train. I loathe travelling by rail. No wonder you're so unkind to me."

Linden had dried her hands and was combing her hair again before she left the cloakroom. But his next remark made her lift her head and stiffen.

"As a matter of fact, it was quite an entertaining journey," he said in an amused tone. "I shared a compartment with a youthful *femme fatale*."

"Oh?" There was a hint of sharpness in his companion's voice. "What do you mean?"

"Well, she started off with a most uninhibited embrace with some lad who was seeing her off, and half an hour later she was flirting with an impressionable American."

By this time Linden's attention was riveted on the conversation outside the window and two spots of angry colour were burning in her cheeks.

"Was she pretty?" the woman enquired, a shade too casually.

"I don't think you'd think so."

"Did she try to flirt with you? Oh, here comes the car. You can tell me all about it on the way home."

Two pairs of footsteps moved away from the window and Linden was left to batten down her temper, but with such a wrathful expression on her face that the cloakroom attendant, coming back from the canteen, looked quite intimidated and scuttled into her cubicle.

A taxi with her luggage on board was waiting for her outside. Linden tipped the porter and gave the address to the driver. She was still trembling with suppressed rage. "Cheer up, miss. It may never happen," said the driver, eyeing her set face in his rear-view mirror.

Linden forced a laugh. "Sorry. I didn't mean to glare."

"Lost in thought, eh?" He braked to allow a car to emerge from the parking enclosure.

It was a gleaming Rolls with a liveried chauffeur at the wheel. And behind, laughing together, were the man named Randal and one of the most beautiful girls that Linden had ever seen. Instinctively she shrank back in her seat, but they were much too absorbed in each other to notice her, and a second later the big car had swung ahead of them and swept through the station gates.

"Are you one of the nurses at the clinic, miss?" the taxi driver asked presently, as they waited at a traffic light.

"What? Oh, yes ... yes, I am," Linden said, hastily gathering her wits.

"I thought so," the driver said sagely. "My daughter had a baby last month. Fine little chap – best part of nine pounds he was. My girl swears by you nurses. Says she'd never have got the same attention in a hospital. Must be a bit of a strain for you, though. Called out at all hours and going without meals and the like."

"Oh, we don't do so badly. It's no worse than working in a hospital," said Linden, distracted from her angry thoughts. "How's your grandson getting on?"

The driver chuckled. "Shouting the house down," he said proudly. "Nothing wrong with his lungs, that's a certainty. Don't please the neighbours too much, you know, but I reckon they just have to put with it for the first month or two. That's the trouble with those council flats – the walls aren't as thick as in the old terrace houses."

"I'm going to live in a council flat," Linden told him. "It's somewhere on the Westleigh Estate."

"Up there, eh? That'll keep you busy," he remarked. "Hasn't been built that long, the Westleigh. It's mostly young couples as have been living in furnished rooms and are just now starting their families. Two or three births every day, I reckon."

"Heavens, I hope not! I shall be working at all hours," Linden said, laughing.

"Well, two or three a week," the driver assured her seriously. He cursed at a jay-walking pedestrian. "I'd heard some of you young ladies were being given council flats," he went on. "Gives you a chance to get more seen to, I suppose, living on the spot."

"Yes, that's the idea – and it's nice to have a place of one's own to relax in," Linden added. "Quite a lot of the midwives live in a staff hostel at the clinic, of course, but I'd rather be independent."

"How d'you get on about meals?" he asked. "Must be a bit discouraging, having to cook your own supper after a heavy day."

"I shall manage, I expect," Linden said cheerfully.

The driver turned the taxi through two tall stone gateposts and along a shrubbery-lined drive. Linden had been told that the town's Central Maternity Clinic was housed in a large Victorian mansion which was no longer suitable for private use. She was unprepared, however, for the beautifully laid out gardens which surrounded the building and, for a moment, she regretted that she would not be living in the staff quarters here. In the heart of the bustling town, the gardens were an oasis of colour and quietude, a pleasant place to relax in on free evenings or after a strenuous afternoon of ante-natal examinations.

As the taxi drew up below the flight of stone steps to the entrance, a dark-haired girl in the trim blue uniform dress of a certified midwife came hurrying out of the front door. She cast a fleeting glance at the taxi and hurried to a small grey saloon car. A moment later she was speeding down the drive.

"Looks like she's had an urgent call," the driver said with a grin as he lifted out the suitcases.

"Probably just a prospective father in a panic," Linden said, laughing. "Just leave my things in the porch, will you, please? I'll be leaving again in a little while."

"Right you are, miss." He did as she asked and accepted his fare and the tip with cordial thanks. "Well, good luck to you in your new job, miss. I daresay I'll see you about. Cheerio."

Linden waved goodbye to him and watched the taxi out of sight. His friendliness and his obviously high regard for the town's midwives seemed a good augury. Pulling down the jacket of her suit and straightening her shoulders, she turned and went into the building.

An hour later, after a cup of coffee and a talk with the Non-Medical Superintendent, Mrs. Langley, she was introduced to Nurse Adams, who was to run her up to her flat.

Jill Adams was a pretty red-haired girl of about the same age as Linden. She had lived in the town all her life and trained at the local hospital. Her district adjoined Linden's area, and when either was off duty, the other would take her calls.

"It will probably take you some time to find your way around," she said, as they left the clinic. "The Westleigh is like a vast rabbit warren — in more ways than one, I might say." Her blue eyes twinkled with laughter and Linden felt sure they were going to get on well together.

"I like Mrs. Langley," she said.

"Oh yes, she's a very good sort," Jill agreed. "She's a widow you know. Her husband was killed in an accident, so she came back to midder to support their twin boys. Of course, she's mostly concerned with admin. now, but she does a delivery occasionally if there's an urgent call when we're all tied up. Incidentally, she's mad on dietetics, so don't let her know if you're living on baked beans and sausages."

The Westleigh Estate lay on the edge of the town and was much as Linden had anticipated: acre upon acre of straight sapling-lined roads with uniform rows of houses and blocks of flats. Most of the gardens were still in a pretty raw state and the gay contemporary curtains at all the windows were further evidence that the district was newly erected.

Her own apartment was on the second floor of a block near the shopping centre. It had been occupied by her predecessor for little more than four months and was furnished with the bare necessities.

"It doesn't look very inviting, but I daresay you can make something of it in time," said Jill, as they walked through the rooms.

"I've got quite a lot of stuff from home coming down tomorrow and some birthday money for extras," Linden explained.

Jill gave her rather a curious glance. Her own background, though certainly not a poor one, was by no means comfortably off. She had four brothers and sisters, two of them still at school, and her choice of nursing as a career – instead of working in a shop or taking up typing and shorthand, which would have enabled her to assist the family budget – had meant additional sacrifices for her parents.

The expensive simplicity of Linden's fashionable suit and the quality of her accessories told Jill that the other girl came from a more affluent milieu. And she could not help wondering why Linden had chosen to take up midwifery, the Cinderella branch of the nursing profession, which, although it was infinitely rewarding to its practitioners, seemed to have little of the glamour which attached to general nursing – at least in the public mind.

When Jill had gone, Linden unpacked her cases and made up the bed. Then she caught a bus into town and bought some food for the weekend.

The following day, a pantechnicon delivered her belongings, including the scarlet motor cycle which she had bought with a small legacy the year before. By

Sunday evening the flat was beginning to look more home-like, and when Jill looked in about eight, a beef casserole was wafting a savoury smell from the oven and Linden was whistling cheerily as she ironed her uniform.

"Mm, that smells good. Whew, I'm whacked!" said Jill, collapsing into a chair.

"Stay and help me eat it," Linden suggested.

"All right — but I'd better ring up home in case Mother's keeping something hot for me."

"How did the case go?" Linden asked, when Jill returned from telephoning.

"It *should* have been as easy as pie," Jill said tiredly. "The trouble was that the girl's mother and mother-in-law had obviously been telling her horror stories. The result was, of course, that, instead of having a perfectly normal delivery, she'd worked herself into a panic and the whole thing took twice as long as it need have done." She sighed. "I sometimes wonder if it's any use teaching relaxation when there are so many older women around who just love to recount their own grue-some experiences."

"Yes, it's maddening, isn't it." Linden agreed sympathetically. "Once or twice I've arrived to find half the street in attendance, busily describing the grimmest details imaginable."

"What have you been doing today?" Jill asked presently, as they started supper.

"I spent this morning trying to get my bearings," Linden said. "I'll have to buy a good street map."

"Oh, by the way, you know your area covers the Heights, I suppose?"

"The Heights?" Linden queried.

"Yes, it's the rather grand residential district on the hill behind this estate. The people up there weren't too pleased when their view was spoilt by all this council development. They're mostly the town's leading citizens and rather snobbish."

"I should think they've had their families by now, haven't they?"

"In the main, yes. One doesn't reach the Heights until one's middle-aged as a rule," Jill said dryly." But we do occasionally have a case up there. You see, the town is very badly off for maternity beds in hospital and the last surviving private nursing home closed down a couple of years ago. Since the N.H.S. got going, it wasn't a paying proposition."

"But even if they can't go into a nursing home, surely the wealthy families don't come to us? I would have thought they'd do the thing in style with the top obstetrician and a resident maternity nurse and what-have-you."

"Yes, they generally do," Jill agreed. "I suppose the reason that young Mrs. Craig is having one of us is that her brother-in-law is on the health committee."

"Who's young Mrs. Craig?" Linden asked, getting up to make the coffee.

"The Craigs are one of our Very Important Families in town. They own the big engineering works down by the river and live in an enormous showplace, at the very top of the Heights. Paula Craig is always called "young Mrs. Craig" because her mother-in-law still rules the roost. Her husband is Andrew Craig, the amateur racing driver. He's very good-looking and of course he has pots of money, but he's bit of a mother's boy, I gather. If I'd been setting my cap at the Craig bank balance, I'd have aimed for Randal."

"Randal?" Linden said sharply.

Jill did not notice her tone. "Yes, he's the elder brother – and a real heart-throb," she explained. "His mother was old Simon Craig's first wife. She was an opera singer, I believe, but she died when Randal was born, so people have almost forgotten her. I've heard that she was ravishingly beautiful, so heaven knows why the old boy picked Adela Craig for his second wife. *She's* a real vinegar bottle,"

"Is Mr. Craig dead?" Linden asked.

"Yes, he had a heart attack about eight years ago. Randal runs the family business and Andrew just plays about with high-powered cars."

After Jill had gone home, Linden had a bath and went to bed. Her mother had given her an alarm-clock-cum-teamaker as a going-away present, and before turning in, she filled the pot and set the alarm for seven.

As she lay in the darkness, listening to a dog barking, her thoughts returned to what Jill had said about the Craigs. So that abominable man on the train was Randal Craig – V.I.P. in the town. Well, Jill might think him a heart-throb, but her own opinion of him was very different. Of all the boorish, self-opinionated . . .

Searching for some more derogatory adjectives to apply to him, she fell asleep.

The first week in any new job was bound to be harassing, and Linden was grateful that only one of the expectant mothers for whom she was responsible was confined during that settling-in period

The baby arrived at four o'clock in the morning, and an hour later, after tucking the infant in its cot and seeing the young mother comfortably settled for sleep, Linden went down to the kitchen for a cup of tea. The baby's grandmother - a sensible, capable woman who had been content to leave her daughter in professional hands - was busy at the stove.

"I'm just frying you some bacon and eggs, Nurse. You'll be hungry after seeing to Janet all this while. There's a nice fire in the sitting-room. Have a minute's sit down. I'll bring this in to you."

"Oh, bless you, Mrs. Lesley," Linden said gratefully. She was not really tired, but she was ravenously hungry.

In the sitting-room, she was surprised to find the young doctor who had been present at the final stages of the delivery. Earlier, absorbed in her task, she had scarcely noticed him, but now she saw that he was a tall, pleasant-faced young man with ruffled fair hair and friendly blue eyes.

Peter Carbury stood up as she entered the room, a mug of coffee in one hand and a pipe in the other.

"Everything O.K., Nurse?" he asked, putting down his pipe to pull forward a chair for her.

"Yes, fine. Mrs. Ellis is having a nap and her husband is gazing at the baby as if he can't quite believe he's real," Linden said, smiling.

The doctor laughed. "They're a nice young couple," he said warmly. "They were in digs for four years before they got this house, so they had quite a wait for the baby." He settled back in a chair and stretched long legs towards the fender. "Well, how do you think you're going to like working here?"

"Oh, very much," Linden answered. "Is it your home town?"

He nodded, re-lighting his pipe. "I've taken on my father's practice," he said, when it was drawing satisfactorily. "It's a pleasant place if you don't mind a fairly quiet life. There's no theatre, of course, and it's pretty dead by ten-thirty, but that doesn't worry me. When I get some spare time I go fishing."

Mrs. Lesley came in with Linden's meal, chatted for a moment, and then hurried back to the kitchen.

"Where do you come from?" the doctor asked.

"London."

"Oh, then you may find the night life a bit slow. There are quite a few club dances and a fair amount of private entertaining goes on, but, as in most provincial towns, people tend to form into cliques with not too much integration."

"As long as there's somewhere to swim and a good library, I shall be happy," Linden replied.

"We can provide those for you. There's an indoor pool and any number of good bathing places along the river, and the library is first rate."

All the time she was eating, he chatted amiably about the town and its amenities, apparently in no hurry to get back to bed. In Linden's experience, most doctors departed within a few minutes of the baby's safe arrival, and she wondered why Doctor Carbury was staying so long.

Half an hour later, after she had packed her equipment in its neat blue canvas bag and told Mrs. Lesley that she would be round in the morning, he accompanied her out to the road.

"Don't you find that a bit exposed in bad weather?" he asked, indicating her motor cycle. "The Corporation will lend you the money to buy a car, you know. You can pay it back on the instalment plan."

"Yes, I know. But I like a motor cycle and there's no problem about garaging it," Linden said, clipping her bag on the carrier.

"The Spartan type, eh? Well, my ancient vehicle is not much more weather-proof, I'll admit."

Linden looked at the battered old station wagon which was parked under the street lamp and smiled. It suited him, she thought. He wouldn't look right driving about in a glossy new saloon, all chrome and stream-lining. He would never be the kind of doctor who was a favourite of hypochondriac matrons, noted for his charming bedside manner. The beds at which he lingered longest would be those of old-age pensioners and sickly children, she guessed.

"Well, goodnight, Nurse – and mind you don't break any speed limits." With a grin and a wave of the hand, he went on his way.

The following afternoon, Linden had a few free

25

hours which she decided to spend shopping for a rug and a lampshade. She had made her purchases and was looking about for a café when she met another of her colleagues, Nurse Lyall. Hearing her intention, Nurse Lyall suggested that they should have tea together.

A fashion parade was in progress in the restaurant of the town's largest store, and the two girls watched with interest as the mannequins strolled past their table in Italian beachwear and gaily printed summer street dresses.

"Fifteen pounds for a shirt! Not on our pay!" Nurse Lyall said wryly. "Now that would suit you, Templar." She indicated an outfit consisting of a rose-pink shirt, matching Bermuda shorts and a cartwheel sun hat trimmed with gold and white shells.

"Unfortunately I'm not going to Nassau this year," Linden said, laughing. She looked towards the entrance where another mannequin was poised to glide forward. But the girl in the white linen suit was not a member of the mannequin team. Instead of parading between the tables, she chose a seat close to them, and as she took off her expensive sunglasses, Linden recognised her as the girl she had glimpsed with Randal Craig on the day of her arrival.

"Now *she* can afford fifteen pounds for a shirt. Money's no object to Melanie Fletcher," Nurse Lyall whispered excitedly.

Linden watched the girl cast her bag and gloves on to the banquette and lift a golden-brown hand to touch her auburn hair. At close view, Melanie Fletcher's looks were as startling as they had seemed that day at the station. Unlike most redheads, she obviously tanned easily, and the combination of her hair and golden skin against the matt whiteness of her suit was extraordinarily arresting. Indeed, Linden noticed that most of the women present were no longer eyeing the mannequins, but gaping with undisguised fascination at Miss Fletcher.

"Who is she?" she asked Nurse Lyall.

"Her father is chairman of the directors of the biscuit factory. She goes to Switzerland every Christmas and she's just come back from Cannes," said Alice Lyall. "I expect that suit she's wearing is a Paris model. She always has marvellous clothes. I say, look at that cigarette case!"

Linden looked, and saw Melanie extracting a cigarette from a thin gold case which appeared to have her initials set in emerald chips. She wondered if the girl was aware that her every movement was the cynosure of the restaurant. Perhaps she was used to being the centre of attention and accepted it as her right.

"They say she's going to marry Randal Craig," Alice went on, in an almost awed tone.

"Do they?" Linden said abstractedly. She was thinking that it would probably be an excellent match: one of those eminently "suitable" marriages in which equal degrees of social standing and affluence counted for so much more than love.

"It must be marvellous to be able to buy anything you fancy," Alice said wistfully, her plump chin cupped in one stubby-fingered hand as she continued to gaze at Melanie.

"She doesn't look particularly radiant," Linden remarked bracingly.

She knew it would be accounted as sour grapes, but she had taken a definite dislike to rich Miss Fletcher. It wasn't that she was envious of the other girl's glamour. Melanie might be outstanding in a provincial town, but in London there were scores of lovely girls, and Linden had never felt at a disadvantage on that account. No: it was something about the faintly petulant droop of that full red mouth and the clipped, unsmiling way with which Melanie gave her order to the waitress.

No one had any right to be so utterly assured, she

thought critically. The other girl had not even bothered to glance round the room. It was as if she knew that the other customers were only local housewives or business girls: none of them sufficiently important to merit the most fleeting attention,

"A penny for them?" Alice said suddenly. "You *were* looking solemn."

"Was I?" Linden smiled. She looked in her purse for the tip. "Let's go, shall we? I've just remembered I want to buy some tights."

During the week Linden had had two letters from Rupert – neither of which said in direct terms that he imagined himself in love with her, but making this very clear by innuendo.

He wrote that he must see her as soon as possible. Couldn't he come down for a couple of nights or better still, would she come home on her first long weekend?

On Sunday afternoon Linden sat down to compose a reply. She was sure that, if she could successfully evade the issue for a couple of months, Rupert would subsequently be grateful to her. He had always been a highly susceptible young man and it was extremely probable that, as soon as some attractive newcomer drifted into his orbit, his sudden regard for Linden would revert to their former uncomplicated friendship.

By the time she had written a long newsy letter with a carefully casual postcript about the impossibility of entertaining friends or going home for several weeks, it was almost tea-time. Putting the kettle on the gas, she slipped a poplin raincoat over her shirt and jeans and slipped out to catch the last post.

She was running back up the stairs, her hair a little damp from the light summer shower, her cheeks pink, when she met Doctor Carbury descending the top flight.

For a moment he seemed not to recognise her out of

uniform, and then he smiled and said, "Hello. Been for a walk?"

"Only to the pillar box. I'm rather expecting a call," Linden said, taking off her coat and fishing in the pocket for her latch key.

The doctor's glance took in the bright yellow shirt and blue linen jeans, a brilliant rose scarf slotted through the waistband. His mouth curved into laughter.

"In my father's time, midwives were mostly elderly dragons with tremendous biceps and a quelling manner," he said, with a twinkle. Linden glanced down at her vivid clothes and smiled, suddenly a little shy.

"I suppose I do look rather gypsyish," she admitted diffidently. "But I spend so much time in uniform that it's nice to have a change."

"Why not? You look very dashing," he agreed. Then, "I'd forgotten you had moved into this flat. I've just been up to your neighbours. Their five-year-old has been a bit off colour and they were worried about polio."

"Is it?" Linden asked anxiously.

"No, just a feverish cold, I think. He's had all the prescribed shots, but I'll keep an eye on him for a day or two."

Through the door, Linden could hear the kettle starting to whistle. "I'm just making tea. Would you like a cup?" she asked.

He hesitated. "Thanks – but I think I'd better get home and catch up with a spot of gardening."

Linden flushed. For a moment she had forgotten their professional relationship and how circumspect – sometimes to the point of absurdity – a doctor had to be.

He must have seen her embarrassment because he said easily, "As a matter of fact I had a cup upstairs. I'm in danger of becoming an addict."

"Yes, I suppose we all drink too much of it," Linden said awkwardly. His remark about gardening had made her realise that he was probably married with a couple of children of his own. She wondered why she had taken it for granted that he was a bachelor.

They said goodbye and she went into the kitchen and turned off the kettle. The window overlooked the road and she could see the station wagon parked there with two small boys writing in the wet dust of the bonnet. They ran off when they saw the doctor coming. and Linden saw him shake a mock-threatening fist at them, but he didn't bother to erase the clumsy lettering before driving away. She smiled to herself, and then, for some reason, she thought of Randal Craig. His car would never be dusty, and streaked with rain, but if it were, she doubted if he would be amused by the childish prank.

On Monday evening she drove up to the Heights for a routine visit to Paula Craig. In marked contrast to the rather bleak aspect of the council estate, the houses here were set well back from the roads and screened by thick shrubberies and high walls. The grass borders between pavement and road were neatly clipped, the gateways all recently painted. Even the gravel on the drives looked freshly swept and the whole neighbourhood gave an impression of sheltered affluence.

Slowing at corners to check her way to Pine Avenue, Linden heard the muted clop of tennis balls. One road she passed was lined with expensive cars. A cocktail party, or perhaps a barbecue supper with dancing on a patio?

Pine Avenue was a cul-de-sac with modern houses and elaborately landscaped gardens on either side. At the far end of the road leading straight through it was a wrought-iron gateway, now standing open. Linden guessed that much of the land outside the gates had once been Craig property but had been sold up for its high building value.

As she drove up the long curving drive, she wondered

if she should have looked for a tradesman's entrance. Her jaunty little bike felt out of place on a carriageway intended for powerful limousines.

The house was a sprawling Victorian mansion which might have looked gloomy and forbidding but for its excellent state of repair. It was surrounded by velvet-smooth lawns and glowing rose beds. Here and there massive green and copper beeches rose out of the flawless turf, and to the right there was the shimmer of water and, beyond it, a shaded white summerhouse.

Linden parked her bike near the low-slung white Renault and went up the shallow steps. Pressing the shining brass bell, she felt a reasonless twinge of nervousness.

The door was opened almost immediately by a maid in coffee uniform with a frilled apron. No European students or slovenly daily helps for the Craigs, Linden thought dryly.

"Is Mrs. Craig in? Mrs. Andrew Craig?" she asked.

"Will you come in, Nurse? I'll see if she can see you," the maid said.

She left Linden standing in a spacious close-carpeted hall and tapped at a door. A moment later she reappeared and said, "Mrs. Craig will see you. What name, please?"

Linden gave her name and the maid returned to the doorway. "Nurse Templar, madam," she announced.

The room was a drawing room of the kind which Linden had seen only in magazine pictures. She had a swift impression of deep chintz-covered couches, of great vases of white lilac and gleaming silver, before she realised that it was not her patient who was waiting for her – but the redoubtable Mrs. Adela Craig.

"Good evening, Nurse. You may sit down." Mrs. Craig looked from a letter she had been reading and indicated a chair close to her own. She was a tall, thin woman in her late fifties with immaculately dressed grey hair and, in Linden's opinion, too much make-up. She was wearing a blue shantung frock—clearly a model—and a triple string of pearls with matching ear-clips.

Her use of the word "may" in asking her visitor to sit down made Linden's mouth tighten, but she met the cold blue eyes with a politely expressionless face.

"It was most unfortunate that Nurse Manton had to leave at this stage of my daughter-in-law's pregnancy, but since it is necessary for you to replace her, I want to explain the position to you," Mrs. Craig said crisply. "No doubt you are surprised that we should engage the services of a district midwife, and of course I should have preferred my daughter-in-law to have her confinement in a London nursing home. However, Mr. Randal Craig is a member of your executive committee and it is therefore a matter of form to utilise local facilities." She paused and gave Linden another appraising glance. "You look very young. You are not a pupil-midwife, are you?"

"I've been fully qualified for two years," Linden said mildly.

"Oh ... well, in any case, our doctor will be in attendance," Mrs. Craig said coolly. "Now I should like you—"

Linden decided that it was time to assert herself. "I'm afraid I haven't a great deal of time to spare this evening, Mrs. Craig," she cut in gently. "If your daughter-in-law is at home, I should like to see her as soon as possible, please."

For several seconds the cold blue eyes met Linden's level grey ones. But before Mrs. Craig could phrase her reply, there was a murmur of voices from outside and two girls came through the french windows. One was Melanie Fletcher and the other was a small, pretty brunette in a pleated maternity dress.

They both stopped talking when they saw Linden, and Paula Craig smiled.

"This is Nurse Templar, Paula," said Mrs. Craig.

Linden rose and young Mrs. Craig smiled again and held out her hand. "Good evening," she said pleasantly. Then over her shoulder to Melanie, "My routine check. I shan't be long."

"Poor darling, what a chore for you. Never mind: it won't last for ever, and then you can consign the infant to its nanny and start making up for lost time," Melanie said in her lazy drawl.

Paula laughed. "I can hardly wait. I feel as if I'd been plodding about in this ghastly tent thing for centuries. Too boring for words!" There was an echo of Melanie's blasé tone in her voice and she gave an exaggerated sigh.

At first Linden thought that, in spite of her charming smile, her patient was going to be as much of a trial as her mother-in-law. But once in her bedroom, Paula's manner changed.

"I'm sorry I missed the relaxation class last week," she said, with obvious sincerity. "My mother-in-law isn't really convinced that the exercises are important and I had to go out to tea with her. But I've been doing them every day at home," she added with enthusiasm.

Linden checked her pulse and blood pressure and asked one or two questions. From the notes she had been given and from her own experience, she judged that Paula Craig was a thoroughly healthy young woman with every expectation of a safe and easy confinement. And what was even more important, she was clearly enjoying her pregnancy and looking forward to the birth.

"Are you in a rush, Nurse? Do come and look at the cradle I've bought," she said, when Linden had written up her notes.

Linden followed her into the adjoining room already equipped as a nursery and decorated in mimosa and white. Admiring the wicker crib with its white

33

nylon draperies and fluffy lemon blankets, Linden wondered why the girl should think it necessary to conceal her excitement before the others. Was she afraid that Melanie would be scornful of her happy anticipation? Or was it her mother-in-law who had forced her into the pretence?

"I'll see you at the class next week," she said, as they parted on the landing.

Having a suspicion that the elder Mrs. Craig might summon her back to the drawing room and demand an account of the examination, she slipped quietly down the stairs and let herself out of the door. She was closing it quietly behind her when a shadow fell across the porch. Turning, she found herself facing Randal Craig.

"Good evening, Nurse. Everything all right?" he asked casually. Then his eyes narrowed and a disbelieving smile tilted his mouth. "Hello!" he said slowly. "This is a surprise. I was wondering if we'd meet again."

CHAPTER TWO

In spite of the effort she made to control it, a slow wave of colour crept up from Linden's throat. Randal's eyes swept over her in unhurried appraisal, taking in the set of her grey beret, the stiff silver-buckled belt that cinched her narrow waist, the sheer grey tights and neat black shoes.

He appeared to have been swimming. A sopping towel was slung over one shoulder and he carried a khaki satchel which was stained with damp. The grey linen beach shirt and faded drill trousers did not diminish that air of complete self-assurance she remembered from the train.

Linden found her voice. "Good evening, Mr. Craig," she said briskly. "Your sister-in-law seems to be very well. Excuse me: I have some more calls to make."

All the way down the steps and across the gravel, she was conscious of him watching her. Praying that the bike would not choose this moment to be temperamental, she clipped her bag to the carrier and pulled on her riding gloves.

A few moments later, pulling out of the gateway, she realised that her mouth was still dry, her heart thumping. It was ridiculous to allow the wretched man to unnerve her, she told herself vexedly. Of course it was only because he had caught her off guard, but even so, it was unlike her to be so stupidly affected by the encounter. She wished she had not shown that she knew who he was. It might have deflated his arrogance slightly to have had to introduce himself.

By the time she had been in Melchester a fortnight, Linden felt happily settled. Had she been in a nine-to-five office job, she might have missed her family and friends in London. But, working irregular hours and finding plenty to do in her erratic spells of leisure, she was never lonely or bored.

There was, in one sense, a good deal of routine work; the weekly relaxation classes, the daily calls to new mothers and their infants, the periodic visits to prospective mothers. But each day offered some fresh interest and experience in the different homes she visited and the various families whom she met.

Jill had told her that the town's midwives averaged about seventy deliveries each during the course of a year, and during her second week, Linden's own total went up to three. Poor Mrs. Lesley, who had been her first patient, was having trouble with baby Charles. After spending the first three days of his existence in a state of profound somnolence, he had woken up with a bang and was roaring the house down. Adjustments were being made to his diet, but Linden suspected that he was suffering from severe colic and that his distracted parents were in for a long ordeal of sleepless nights and harassed days.

At the end of the fortnight, she had forty-eight hours off duty. On Sunday afternoon she packed a towel and some sandwiches and walked down to the river for an afternoon of swimming and sunbathing.

There were gangs of youths and girls all along the bank and a number of portable radios playing. Linden strolled along the towpath until she was some distance beyond the last group of youngsters and chose a dappled stretch of grass beneath a tree. On the other side of the river there were houses with long gardens sloping down to the water. As she took off her sandals, she could see a man dozing in a deck chair with a Panama hat tilted over his face, and in another garden, a small boy romping with a terrier.

As she slipped off her dress and fastened the halter of

her swimsuit, Linden thought what an attractive and serene view it was, and how typical of summer Sunday afternoons all over the country. She was suddenly intensely conscious of the inestimable value of peace and had a momentary pang of terror in case it should all be disrupted before she had time to experience all that life could offer.

Thrusting this sombre thought aside, she fastened her hair into a tail and walked through the warm grass to the edge of the river. The gently flowing water was almost tepid and, coming up from her dive, she blinked at the clear blue sky and was happy and carefree again.

She had been in the water about half an hour and was back-stroking leisurely along near the far bank when someone called out to her. Treading water, she looked round to see Doctor Carbury waving to her from one of the gardens

"I thought I recognised that hair," he said, as she came nearer to him. "You seem to be having a good time."

Linden grasped the side of a punt which was moored to an old tree stump and smiled up at him. "I am. What are you doing here?"

"I live here. My mother's just made tea. Would you like to come up and have some with us?"

"In my swimsuit?"

"Why not? We can lend you a wrap."

"What about my things? Is it safe to leave them?"

"I'll paddle over and fetch them for you." Before she could object, he had cast off the punt. Linden hauled herself out of the water and waited for him to come back. She hoped his mother would not mind his bringing up a wet guest.

"Here you are." He tossed the towel to her and secured the punt again.

They walked up the slanting lawn, Linden feeling

rather self-conscious in her scanty suit. "What lovely rockeries! How on earth do you find time to keep them in order?" she asked.

He grinned. "My mother does the skilled work. I just mow and dig occasionally."

Part of the upper garden was screened by a rose-covered trellis. As they passed through an arch, Linden saw that a white-haired woman was sitting by a tea table, knitting.

"This is my mother, Nurse Templar," the doctor said, as the woman looked up from her work and smiled at him. "I found Nurse drifting downstream and thought she'd like some tea," he explained.

"Why, of course. How do you do, my dear," Mrs. Carbury said warmly. "Do sit down. Oh, don't mind damping the chairs. My son doesn't. Peter, fetch another cup, will you, dear?"

Linden's first impression of Mrs. Carbury was that she was the complete antithesis of Adela Craig. They were about the same age and both tall, slim women – but there the resemblance ended. Constance Carbury had kindness and humour in every line of her charming weathered face. She looked exactly what she was: a throughly contented woman who found life in the middle years as rich as it had ever been.

"And how do you like Melchester, Miss Templar?" she asked, folding her knitting and putting it on a stool.

"Very much indeed, thank you. I – I hope you don't mind my arriving like this. I'm not really fit to pay any calls," Linden said diffidently.

"Oh, don't let that worry you, my dear," Mrs. Carbury assured her laughingly. "I've three sons, and ever since they could talk they've been issuing invitations to all kinds of people. When Tom was nine I found him entertaining a most dubious-looking tramp in the kitchen. Between them they'd eaten most of the cakes I'd baked for an important tea party. A pretty girl in a bathing suit is quite unexceptionable, I assure you."

"What on earth did you do – about the tramp, I mean?" Linden enquired, intrigued.

"I gave the poor man half-a-crown and a pair of my husband's gardening trousers – and I explained to Tom that I didn't mind him bringing his friends home as long as he asked permission to give them the freedom of the pantry," Mrs. Carbury said with a twinkle. "Now Peter was always finding stray kittens and nestlings. I remember once he brought in an invalid worm. He wanted his father to give it an injection, but we had to make do with nursing it in a box of earth for several days. He was very upset when it disappeared."

Peter Carbury grinned. "She may as well hear the full story. I daresay she's been given a long list of all my present failings. The first thing the nurses do is to warn newcomers what a difficult lot of cranks they've got to put up with. Isn't that so, Nurse?"

Linden laughed. "I wouldn't put it quite like that. Naturally it's a help to know if a doctor likes things done in a particular way!"

"What bees we've got in our bonnets, you mean. Here - you'd better slip this on or you may catch cold. Or you can nip indoors and change if you'd prefer."

"Oh, no – I'll be fine," Linden said, accepting the towelling robe he was holding out for her. It was made for a six-footer with a proportionate breadth of shoulder and completely enveloped her, but she felt more presentable in it.

The doctor's tea proved to consist of fluffy home-made scones, a big bowl of strawberries and cream and a slice of delicious layer cake.

"I couldn't possibly – I feel half a stone fatter already," Linden said breathlessly, when her hostess urged her to have some more.

"A very good thing if you were – I expect you half

starve yourself," the doctor said dryly. "It's a pity you girls aren't issued with milk and vitamins like the pregnant mums. To the devil with all this dieting. You need plenty of nourishing food when you're working hard."

"But I don't diet!" Linden protested. "I eat as much as I like."

He eyed her sceptically. "I know: a cup of tea for breakfast and a tin of soup for lunch."

"Everyone hasn't your voracious appetite, Peter," his mother remarked amusedly.

"Perhaps not. But I'm convinced that a lot of women are persistently run down because they refuse to eat sensibly," he said seriously.

"Well, I'm as strong as a horse," Linden said cheerfully.

"Heaven help the girls my sons marry. They'll expect the wretched creatures to live in the kitchen," his mother said, smiling.

"Which will be entirely your fault for bringing us up to be gourmands," the doctor replied, with a grin. "If you hadn't forced that second slice of cake on me, I could be going down for a swim. Now I'll have to wait half an hour for it to digest."

The two women smiled at each other, because he had eaten the cake with all the relish of a hungry schoolboy.

"That reminds me, I must go and deal with the supper. Why don't you spend the evening with us, my dear?" Mrs. Carbury suggested to Linden.

"Yes, good idea," the doctor agreed. "You haven't a date laid on, have you?"

"Well, no. But . . ."

"That's settled, then. Tom and Ruth will be back about eight. Ruth is my brother's fiancée – I think you'll like her."

"If you're sure I won't be intruding?" Linden said shyly.

"Of course not – we're glad to have you. It always takes a while to get to know people in a strange town, particularly when you don't get your free time at regular hours."

"Oh, well, that's just an occupational hazard," Linden said, untying her hair and shaking it out to dry.

The doctor regarded her thoughtfully. "I would have thought it rather a major disadvantage in your case."

"Why in my case?"

He produced his pipe and began to fill it, pressing the flakes into the bowl with capable square-tipped fingers. Watching him, Linden remembered how she had noticed Randal Craig's hands that day in the train and wondered if he was a doctor.

"Aren't dates and dances a pretty important part of any girl's life?" he asked casually.

"Yes ... I suppose they are," Linden agreed. "But we don't sacrifice *all* social life, you know." She bent to flick an ant off her bare brown ankle and her hair swung forward about her face. She straightened and brushed it back "If what you really mean is 'Do we worry about missing chances of meeting men and getting married?' – the answer is 'No'. Obviously, there are times when it's very disappointing not to have the evening off. But I suppose most of us feel that anybody worth while will just accept the situation. Anyway, that's how *I* feel about it."

The doctor gave her another of those intent looks, but did not reply immediately.

"Yes, I suppose that's the only way you can look at it," he said at length. "A doctor is in much the same boat, of course. The snag with us is that we don't retire when we marry. A girl may be prepared to stand the inconvenience for a few months, but it's something

41

else to put up with emergency calls for the rest of your life."

"The answer is to marry a nurse," Linden said, smiling. The words were no sooner out than a fiery blush suffused her face. Oh, what a fool thing to say! He might think . . .

Peter finished filling his pipe and looked up at her. For a moment his expression was so cool that Linden could have sunk into the earth. Then the lines beside his eyes began to crinkle and he leaned back in his chair and roared with laughter.

"Don't look so embarrassed, girl," he said, delightedly. Linden managed a weak smile. If only she did not colour up so easily. That always made matters worse.

"You know, that first evening we met, I was slightly intimidated," he went on, still looking very much amused. "You were so extremely self-possessed I was afraid you were one of those potential-matron types. It's reassuring to find you're not all starch and efficiency."

Linden blinked at him. She had not been aware of any unusual briskness in her manner on the night in question.

Inside the house the telephone began to ring, and a few moments later Mrs. Carbury appeared at one of the windows.

"It's for you, Peter," she called.

The doctor groaned and pulled himself up from his chair. "Bang goes my lazy evening," he said wryly. "Look, do you want to swim again?"

Linden shook her head.

"Then come indoors and change. If I am called out, it may not take too long, and meanwhile you can probably give Mother a hand with supper."

For once, however, the call was not from a patient, and when Linden had dressed she found him sitting on the kitchen table while her hostess garnished an aspic jelly.

It proved to be a most agreeable evening. Tom Carbury was as likeable as his brother and his petite, vivacious fiancée – a teacher at the local grammar school – kept them all amused with her account of a recent school trip to France.

It was after ten o'clock when the doctor drove Linden home.

"Don't bother to get out," she said quickly, as he pulled up outside the flats. "I have enjoyed myself, Doctor Carbury. Thank you very much for having me."

"It's been a pleasure, Nurse Templar," he said, smiling.

Linden reached for the door handle, but turned it the wrong way.

"Look, as you're now a friend of the family, I think we might dispense with formalities when we're both off duty," he said, reaching across to unfasten it for her. "You know my name, but I don't know yours."

"Oh ... it's Linden."

"Goodnight, Linden."

"Goodnight ... Peter."

She slipped out of the car, waved and ran across the grass.

"There! Such a lovely clean boy! Now don't be impatient. You'll have your lunch in a minute."

Linden propped the week-old baby comfortably on her arm and brushed his blond floss into a neat cockscomb.

"There you are, Mrs. Anderson. You'd better feed him before he dies of starvation," she said laughingly, handing him back to his proud mother.

"I'm dreading having to bath him. I'm sure I'll drop him," the girl said anxiously.

Linden unfastened the gauze mask she had worn while attending to the baby. "It's not really so difficult

43

once you've had some practice," she said encouragingly. "You can try your hand at it tomorrow. I expect you'll manage very well."

She began to clear the bath things and discarded clothing, noticing the delicate embroidery on the hand-tucked nightgown and the softness of the tiny knitted vest. This baby was one of the lucky ones: welcomed and cherished and assured of loving care. But an hour or so earlier she had been visiting a very different household. There, the new arrival was just an additional burden to its worn, tired mother. Soothing its fretful whimper while three older children played in the unkempt room, Linden had thought that, even in its first days of existence, that baby seemed to sense that its life was going to be a struggle.

Carrying the bath through to the kitchen, she found a neighbour making tea.

"Going on lovely, isn't he, Nurse? the woman said warmly.

"Yes, he's a bonny little chap," Linden agreed.

She tipped the water into the sink and glanced idly through the window. Then her fingers tightened on the pale yellow plastic. A sleek grey convertible had just drawn up at the garden gate, and the man at the wheel was Randal Craig.

"That's a posh car!" the neighbour said, over her shoulder.

"Yes, isn't it?" Instinctively Linden drew back behind the curtain.

"Someone for next door," the neighbour said, watching eagerly. "Wonder what he's after? Can't be no relation of the old people, I shouldn't think. P'raps he's from the pension office. Must be one of the head ones, if he is."

Linden went back to the sitting room to write up her report. Presently the neighbour followed with the tea tray.

"We've just seen ever such a nob calling on your

neighbours, Mrs. Anderson," she announced excitedly. "Who d'you suppose it would be?"

"Oh, someone from the council, I expect. Old Mrs. Kent did tell me she'd written up to them," the girl said absently, much too absorbed in her baby to pay more than a fleeting attention to events in the outside world.

"No wonder the rates is so high – with them running round in them big cars," the neighbour said acidly. "Still he was a good-looking young fellow. Maybe I'll write up myself and have him come calling on me." She winked at Linden and went back to the kitchen, laughing at her own wit.

Linden drank her tea and watched the baby, tipsy with milk, being winded. Then she tucked him down in his crib and advised Mrs. Anderson to take a nap.

As she let herself out of the house, the adjoining front door was opened. Linden hesitated, torn between ducking back indoors and sprinting down the path. But it was already too late. Before she had decided what to do, Randal Craig had stepped out of the next door and seen her.

"Good morning, Nurse," he said pleasantly. "Just the person I want to see. Can you spare a moment?"

Depriving Linden of the chance to make some quick excuse, he turned and said goodbye to the old lady who was with him.

"Now don't you worry, Mrs. Kent. I promise to look into the whole matter and see if we can help you out. It shouldn't take more than a day or two and then I'll come up and tell you what can be done. Good morning."

The door closed behind him, and he turned to Linden. "You know, I haven't quite got used to the idea of your being a nurse," he said, smiling at her. "When we travelled down from London together, it was the last job I would have ascribed to you."

45

"Really?" Linden said frostily. "How can I help you, Mr. Craig?"

"You start by dropping that super-professional manner just a little," he said dryly. "I wanted to have a word with you about my sister-in-law. But if I've chosen an inconvenient time . . ."

"Is Mrs. Craig unwell?" Linden cut in quickly.

"No, she seems to be extremely fit. It's not her health that I'm concerned about."

"Then how can I help you?" Linden asked, puzzled.

"Let's talk in the road, shall we?" he suggested.

They walked down the path and he reached over the hedge and swung the gate open for her.

"For some weeks I've suspected that Paula isn't very happy," he said seriously. "I've mentioned it to her husband and my stepmother, but neither of them appear to have noticed anything. Yesterday I found her crying. She said she was just feeling depressed and begged me not to say anything to anyone. I realise, of course, that women do have odd moods at these times, but I'm still rather anxious about her. I wondered if, when you come up to see her again you could make some tactful enquires. She might confide to you what she won't tell us."

Linden studied the clasp of her case for a moment. "Can you think of any reason why she should be upset, Mr. Craig?" she asked.

"None at all – unless it could be that she's nervous about her confinement."

Linden shook her head. "No, I don't think it's that," she said thoughtfully. "She may not show it too much, but I think she's very excited and pleased about the baby. As you say, women do have strange moods, especially in the last few weeks. But I'll certainly do what I can to find out the trouble."

"Thank you. I hope you're successful," he said gravely.

Perhaps, if this had been their first meeting, Linden might have liked him. Without the glint of challenge in his eyes and that faintly cynical tilt at the corner of his mouth, he looked younger and more approachable. For a moment she forgot that she had excellent reason to dislike him. A man who concerned himself with the problems of old-age pensioners and worried in case his brother's wife had a secret fear could not be quite as egocentric as she had supposed.

He walked to the curb with her and watched her fasten her bag on the carrier.

"Have you been riding this long?" he asked, examining the motor cycle's controls.

"About a year."

"H'm, it isn't very practical in the winter, is it?"

"I find it quite satisfactory with a good oilskin cape," Linden replied.

"What happens if something goes wrong when you're on an urgent call?" There was a definite note of criticism in his voice.

"I have it serviced regularly, so it shouldn't go wrong," she said evenly. "Don't you approve of motor cycles, Mr. Craig?"

"As fine-weather runabouts, I think they're very good value. I don't consider them a particularly reliable vehicle for your work," he said coolly.

Linden looked over his shoulder at the streamlined coupé. "Even if I drove a Jensen, I could still have an occasional breakdown," she pointed out.

His mouth twitched. "Oh, certainly – but the odds are somewhat shorter. You know, I suppose, that the local authority would help you buy a car?"

"Oh, certainly – but I don't happen to want one," Linden retorted crisply. "Unless, of course, you use your influence to make them compulsory."

His eyes narrowed, but not before she had seen the flicker of anger in them.

"I mustn't keep you any longer," he said with icy formality. "Good morning, Nurse."

Watching him stride away to his car, Linden knew a momentary regret for her impetuous remark. Whatever her personal opinion of him, she had had no right to resort to sarcasm. On the other hand, *he* had had no right to be so arbitrary. She wondered if he would report her for gross impertinence, or ask for another nurse to be put on his sister-in-law's case. It was probably the first time in his life that anyone had dared to answer him back.

But although she tried to dismiss the encounter from her mind, Linden felt twinges of conscience all the rest of that day. Like most people who very rarely lose their tempers, on the infrequent occasions when this did happen she invariably suffered a good deal of remorse afterwards — however much justification there might have been for the lapse.

The following afternoon, she called at the Craig house, and this time was taken immediately to her patient, who was resting on a wicker lounging couch on the terrace behind the house.

As Linden approached, a young man rose from his chair and Paula said, "Hello, Nurse. This is my husband. Darling, this is my new nurse."

Linden's introduction to Andrew Craig reminded her of the holiday advertisements in the glossy magazines, in which lovely girls and magnificent young men swept over a deep blue sea on water-skis round the pool of some luxury liner. Of medium height but superb physique, his blond hair falling in an engaging forelock over one sun-bleached eyebrow, Paula Craig's husband was so different from his stepbrother that it was difficult to believe there was any relationship between them.

After chatting to Linden for some minutes, he smiled down at his wife and said, "Well, I'll leave you to your mysteries. If you don't mind, sweetheart, I think I'll go for a run. I shan't be late back."

"Yes, do go, darling. I wish I could come with you," Paula said regretfully. It was clear that she was wildly in love with him.

"So do I, my pet – but we daren't disobey Big Brother's orders," he said, with a laugh. "Take care of yourself. 'Bye, Nurse."

When he had gone, Paula shifted restlessly on the couch and pushed away her sewing with a gesture of suppressed impatience. "I wish it didn't take so long to have a baby," she said, with a sigh. "Andrew's terribly sweet about it, but I'm sure he's awfully bored by my never being able to go out with him – in the car, I mean."

"I should think a drive would do you good, as long as you didn't go too fast," Linden said pleasantly, preparing to check her blood pressure.

"That's the trouble. Andrew's a marvellous driver – he wanted to take it up professionally. But he adores speed, so Randal has forbidden him to take me out until after the baby comes. I've told him it doesn't frighten me, and Andrew's never had an accident yet, but once Randal makes up his mind you just can't budge him an inch."

"Well, even the best drivers do have accidents – so perhaps it's a wise precaution," Linden suggested. "And you've only another three weeks to go if the baby is punctual."

"Yes, thank goodness," Paula agreed, more cheerfully. "Of course, in a way, I suppose I shall be more tied then than I am now. My mother-in-law wants us to have a nanny, but I'm not sure that I'm too keen and I know Randal doesn't approve."

Randal seems to run everybody's lives round here, Linden reflected rather grimly.

Aloud she said, "Most people would say that if you

49

can afford a nanny, you'd be mad not to have one. Babies make an enormous amount of work and they can be frightfully wearing at times. On the other hand, if you have a professional nurse you lose a lot of the fun and tend to feel only half a mother. At least, that's what I gather from people who've tried both. What does your husband think about it?"

"Oh, Andrew doesn't mind either way, as long as I'm happy," Paula said airily.

"Why does Mr. Craig disapprove?" Linden asked guardedly.

"He thinks children don't feel so secure if they're looked after by a nurse most of the time. I think he remembers his own childhood. It wasn't a very happy one. I should think he was an odd little boy, and after Andrew was born he probably got pushed into the background a good deal."

She stopped and looked a little uncomfortable, as if conscious that she had been talking very freely to someone who was still almost a stranger.

Linden popped a thermometer in her mouth and glanced round the attractive garden. So Randal resented having had to take a back seat and is making up for it now by being the family despot, she thought coldly. She could pity any child who was ousted from favour as consequence of a second marriage; but she could not feel much compassion for a grown man who revenged himself by inflicting his will on others.

When she had concluded her examination, she accepted Paula's offer of an iced drink and led the conversation into less personal channels for a time.

"Under that tree will be a good spot for the baby's naps," she said presently, indicating a spreading copper beech across the lawn. "Are you living here permanently, Mrs. Craig? Or just while the baby is coming?"

"It isn't really settled yet," Paula said vaguely. "You see we've only been married a year and we came

50

here after our honeymoon to give us time to look for a house or a building site. Somehow, what with the baby starting so soon and one thing and another, we've let our plans slide. It's very convenient to be here just now because I don't feel much like housework and it's so difficult, getting help."

Linden had the impression that she was putting forward someone else's arguments in favour of the arrangement. She had seen the difficulties that living with relations could present in less affluent circumstances. She was inclined to the view that, even in these surroundings, it was not a good thing for young couples to share a home. Perhaps this was the cause of Paula's secret depression: that, deep down, she longed for a house of her own.

They were discussing the rival merits of modern and period houses, when Paula waved to someone across the garden. Turning, Linden saw Randal Craig coming towards them. She mastered an impulse to make a rapid departure, and waited for him to reach them.

Paula, not knowing that they had already met, introduced them. From Randal's response there was no means of telling whether he was still annoyed or had completely forgotten their last meeting.

"I thought Andrew was at home this afternoon," he said, when both women had refused his offer of a cigarette.

"He was: but when Nurse Templar came he decided to go out for a spin," Paula explained

He made no comment, but Linden felt that the information displeased him.

Presently she rose to leave, and as she had anticipated, Randal said he would see her out. They walked round the side of the house, but he did not immediately question her about Paula's well-being, and his silence made it even more difficult for Linden to nerve herself to say what she felt she must.

51

"I'm afraid I was not very polite to you the other morning, Mr. Craig," she began uncertainly. "I – I apologise."

He glanced down at her with a rather sardonic gleam in his eyes. "That's very handsome of you, Nurse Templar," he said dryly. "Let's forget the matter, shall we? Did you find out if anything *is* worrying Paula?"

Linden hesitated. "No ... no, I'm afraid I didn't," she said finally. "I think, if she was upset, it was probably just a passing mood. The last few weeks can seem interminable, you know, and no doubt she misses being able to go out with her husband as much as she'd like."

"H'm ... well, if you think that's all it was," he said, sounding doubtful.

In fact, Linden thought there was a good deal more to the matter. But she felt that her talk with Paula had been too inconclusive for her to commit herself, and also that, however genuine his concern might be, Randal Craig was not the best person to whom to pass on her conjectures.

At this point the maid came out of the house to tell him he was wanted on the telephone and, excusing himself to Linden, he disappeared.

The next few days were so busy that Linden had little time to dwell on the conflict of personalities in the Craig household. Two of the other nurses were on temporary sick leave – one with a sprained wrist and the other with a mild attack of food poisoning – so their work had to be divided among their colleagues. Inevitably, several infants in Linden's and Jill's areas were born within hours of each other and, by the time the sudden spate of births was over, both girls were tired to the bones.

"I wonder what would happen if *we* went on strike?" Jill said cuttingly, as she glanced through a three-day-old newspaper and drank some sweet, strong tea at the clinic one afternoon.

Linden laughed. "I doubt if the country would come to a standstill, but there'd certainly be a major panic," she said, rubbing a stiffness in one shoulder.

"I'd like to see some of these wretched strikers trying their hand at our job," Jill said bitterly. "They might realise how lucky they are to be able to watch TV every night and lie in bed on Sunday mornings." She threw the paper aside. "I wish someone would ask me to marry him! I'm sure the production side is much easier than the delivery service."

"Well, it's Leap Year. Why don't you seize the initiative?" Linden suggested teasingly.

"I would – if I could find a suitable victim," Jill said, with an exaggerated sigh. "Now if I'd stayed in general and spent my time tripping round the men's surgical ward, I'd probably be married by now."

She paused to powder her nose and apply fresh lipstick. "The trouble with this job is that the only men we meet are harassed husbands and much-married G.P.s. With the exception of Peter Carbury, I can't think of anyone who's worth a second glance, and unfortunately he doesn't react to my subtle charm. How about you? Did he murmur any sweet nothings when you were coping with the Baxter baby?"

"They sounded more like smothered curses," Linden said, grinning. "We were all at a pretty low ebb by five o'clock in the morning. The only lively members of the party were the baby and Mrs. Baxter's ancient grandmother, who was hovering outside the door and muttering about how she'd had thirteen without any of this new-fangled nonsense. But I doubt if any of hers were whopping ten-pounders."

They left the clinic together, cheered by the break for gossip. Halfway home, Linden met Jill's unsuspecting heart-throb in his shabby car. He waved to her to stop and backed along the road till they were level.

"Got the evening off? How about coming over for a swim? It will probably do you more good than putting your feet up," he suggested. "Come to supper. My mother's been asking about you."

Linden had planned to shampoo her hair and catch up with some ironing, but the prospect of an evening by the river was more attractive. She accepted his invitation and hurried back to the flat to change out of uniform.

While she was slipping into a cool pink and white gingham shirtwaister, the telephone rang and she groaned. But mercifully it was not another job of work but a long-distance call from London.

"Hello? Linden? This is Rupert. How are you?"

Linden grimaced at herself in the mirror. Poor Rupert! She had almost completely forgotten him in the week's bustle of activity.

The pips had gone three times before she felt justified in pleading an urgent engagement, and as she snatched up her bag and ran down the stairs she wondered anxiously if his feelings were deeper than she had imagined. Still, it was less than a month since he had kissed her goodbye. He had once laughingly said that six weeks was his customary time-span for falling in and out of love.

Riding round to the Carburys', she remembered what Jill had said about their being doomed to spinsterdom. It had been meant as a joke, but, thinking about it more seriously, Linden realised that it was a long time since she had considered marriage as anything more than a distant probability. Not since she had thought herself in love with a medical student – and that was way back in her junior "pro" days, she discovered with a slight sense of shock.

As Peter had promised, a leisurely swim in the river

and an appetising supper were much more relaxing than an evening spent by herself. Lying back in a garden chair, watching the sun go down and listening to some soothing records on the portable record player, Linden found all her tiredness had gone.

She wondered what Randal Craig was doing this evening and then caught herself up with a jerk. Why on earth was she thinking about *him*?

A chuckle from Peter made her turn her head enquiringly.

"I've been watching you for about five minutes and I must say I'm intrigued to know what you're thinking about," he said, smiling at her. "You started by looking as if you were dropping off to sleep, and then you gave a very long sigh and then a startled look and finally a fierce scowl."

"Did I?" Linden was glad of the fading light that made her heightened colour less noticeable. "I can't really remember what I was thinking about," she said untruthfully.

There was a distance of about two feet between their chairs and Linden had been absently plucking at the grass beside her. Suddenly Peter reached out and took hold of her wrist.

"How do you manage to keep your hands like this when they're always in water or disinfectant?" he asked, looking at the smooth brown skin and well-kept nails which she had time to paint with a clear pink varnish before coming out. His touch was quite impersonal, but the contact made Linden feel oddly restive.

"Oh, I cream them every night to stop them chapping. If I'm feeling very vain, I sleep in cotton gloves," she said lightly. "Of course we can never have those elegant long nails like fashion models."

He let go of her hand and reached for his mug of beer. "Well, you aren't the scarlet-taloned type, are you?" he said, looking amused.

"I don't think I'm any type at all," Linden answered. "At least I can never place myself in those 'Which are you' quizzes. I'm certainly not an exotic orchid type, and only an half an outdoor girl — I loathed games at school — so that leaves the brisk, capable careerist or the born housewife type, and they don't fit either."

"I should say you're a mixture of outdoor girl and housewife," he said thoughtfully.

Linden laughed. "Which sounds the most ghastly of the lot!" she said wryly. But somehow her amusement was only surface-deep, and she felt an odd prick of irritation that he should see her as that particular combination.

She had a sudden mental picture of Melanie Fletcher, of that beautiful imperious face and wilful red mouth. No one would ever dub Melanie the open-air-cum-kitchen-sink type. Her outdoor activities would be winter-sporting at St. Moritz or sunning at Cap d'Antibes. She would be a hostess rather than a housewife: presiding over candle-lit dinner tables, not getting hot and flustered in a two-by-four kitchenette with the gravy burning and the soufflé sinking and a frilly pinafore over some off-the-peg dress.

I resent her, Linden discovered with surprise. Not just Melanie herself, but the kind of woman she represents. Women whom men don't take for granted, who aren't forced into a rut of domestic chores, women who have time to be exciting and stimulating.

Aware that Peter had begun to talk about his holiday plans, Linden listened with one ear while a curious dissatisfaction with herself and life in general niggled at the back of her mind.

Perhaps it was merely that she was more tired than she had realised — although a spell of rush work didn't usually leave her a prey to gloomy moods. Or perhaps it was just a fit of that nameless longing for something new to happen that usually attacked her in the first soft week of spring but which could flare up suddenly at other times of year. Yes, a delayed bout of spring fever – that must be what it was!

"... so I thought we'd motor south from Brussels and explore the Ardennes country. Have you been there?" Peter asked.

Linden hastily roused herself from the unwonted introspection.

"Er ... no ... no, I haven't," she said quickly.

His eyes crinkled at the corners. "You've been day-dreaming," he said gently. "I don't think you've heard a word I said."

She flushed. "I'm sorry, Peter. I didn't mean to be rude. I – I think I must be getting sleepy."

"Shall I take you home?"

"Oh, no, I'm not as tired as all that – unless you want to get rid of me," she said, smiling.

"Of course not. I expect Mother will produce some coffee presently." He knocked out his pipe and finished the last of the beer. "Are you engaged, Linden?" he asked suddenly.

"Why, no! What made you think I was?"

"Oh, nothing ... I just wondered."

"You're not very observant." She waved her ringless left hand.

"You might keep your ring for special occasions," he pointed out. Then, glancing about in search of his tobacco pouch, he said casually, "Those faraway moods are a bad sign, you know."

"A bad sign?" she queried.

"Or a good one – depends how you look at it. They're usually the early symptoms of the condition known as Love."

Linden drew in her breath. "Are they?" she said, after a moment. "Well, I don't think I'm sickening for anything."

57

"One doesn't – until one's laid low," he said dryly.

Linden bent to fiddle with the strap of her sandal. "Wrong diagnosis, Doctor," she said lightly. "I'm always a bit absent-minded when I'm pleasantly drowsy and full of good food."

But later, getting ready for bed, she remembered that snatch of conversation and wondered why, for the space of a few seconds, a feeling that was almost like panic had gripped her. Oh, nonsense, she thought briskly. I'm not in love with poor old Rupert and I've only met two bachelors since I've been here. Peter is nice and I like him enormously – but that's just friendship. The only other man is Randal Craig and I'd certainly never fall for anyone of *that* type.

The very absurdity of such a notion made her laugh out loud, and she went to bed having dismissed the topic from her mind and with her thoughts on the safer subject of what she had to do next day.

Linden was woken up the next morning by the concerted clamour of the alarm clock and the telephone. Struggling out of the bedclothes, she silenced the alarm with one hand and lifted the receiver with the other.

"Melchester 2173?" The operator's voice came hollowly from some distant exchange.

Oh lord, not Rupert again! Not at this hour!

But it was her father's voice that came over the line a few seconds later.

"Linden? This is Father. Sorry if I woke you up, dear, but I wanted to be sure of catching you. Are you off duty tonight?"

"I don't know. What's the matter? Is mother ...?"

"Mother's fine. Now listen ..."

In the rather gruff voice he always used on the telephone, Mr. Templar explained that he was making an unexpected business trip to the north and had thought of making a detour en route in order to spend a night in Melchester.

"Oh, Poppy darling, that would be lovely – but I haven't anywhere to put you," Linden exclaimed.

"That doesn't matter. I'll put up at an hotel. Perhaps you could book a room for me before you go out. I've looked in the A.A. book. The Carlton sounds a suitable place and we can have dinner there."

They chatted for a few more moments and Linden promised to do her best to get the evening off. Then the pips sounded and Mr. Templar, who disapproved of prolonged telephone conversations, rang off.

Fortunately none of Linden's cases started labour during the day, and, having let the clinic know where they could reach her if necessary, she was able to hurry into town soon after six. The Carlton was one of the two leading hotels in Melchester and she had changed into a simple dinner dress of dark green jersey with a low scooped-out neckline and finely pleated skirt.

Leaving her bike in the hotel park, she walked round to the main entrance and found her father reading a paper in one of the deep armchairs in the entrance lounge.

"Well, you look very fit, my dear," Mr. Templar said approvingly, when they had kissed each other. He was a tall, lean man with crisp grey hair and rather beetling eyebrows.

"Of course I'm fit, Poppy. What did you expect? A wasted wraith?" Linden said teasingly.

"I think your mother's been a bit concerned about you. As a matter of fact it was she who suggested I should spend a night here. I'm to telephone her before dinner and assure her that you're all right."

"Oh, Mummy's hopeless. She refuses to admit that any of us has grown up," Linden said affectionately. "I'm surprised she didn't tell you to make sure I was washing behind my ears or to give me a good dose of syrup of figs."

Her father took out his cigarette case and offered it to her. "To tell you the truth, I find it rather hard to realise that you're a grown woman myself," he admitted wryly. "Makes me feel quite an old stager."

"Nonsense. You don't look at all elderly and staid like most people's fathers," Linden said admiringly.

This was true. Neither of her parents looked their age, and when she was working in London and had sometimes taken her friends home, Linden had been amused to discover that her father was still capable of having an effect on girls in their twenties.

"If any of my patients should see me here, they'll probably think I've got a wealthy sugar-daddy," she said, with a grin.

"I suppose that's a hint that you're expecting a slap-up dinner, is it?" he said, with a twinkle. "Well, since you're no longer a permanent strain on my pocket, I suppose I should indulge you to a reasonable extent. Look, I'll call your mother now, and then it's off my conscience. I expect she'll want to speak to you, but I'm certainly not paying a two-hour telephone bill, and I know what you two are once you get started."

"Well, give her my love and tell her I'm putting on weight," Linden said gaily. "Shall I order some drinks while I'm waiting?"

She was sipping a glass of sherry and enjoying the discreet opulence of her surroundings, when the bell boy hurried forward to open the main door and a party of people came in. Linden glanced towards them, and then looked again.

There were three women and four men. One woman and three of the men were strangers to her. The others were Melanie Fletcher, Adela Craig and her stepson. If they were having dinner here, the newcomers would have to pass her chair, and so, after noting that Melanie was looking ravishing in a dress of stiff bronze silk with a pale mink jacket slung over her shoulders, Linden quickly attended to tipping ash into the tray. Not that any of them were likely to recognise her. People like the Craigs and their friends would never expect to find their underlings – and presumably she was included in this category – encroaching on their social preserves. And if such a thing did happen, they would probably choose to ignore it.

The rustle of silk came nearer and Linden caught a drift of expensive French scent. She reached for a magazine.

"Good evening, Miss Templar."

Conscious that the whole party had paused to see whom he was speaking to, Linden looked up to find Randal Craig smiling at her.

"Good evening, Mr. Craig," she said coolly. Without looking beyond him, she could sense that both Mrs. Craig and Melanie were surveying her with faintly arched eyebrows.

"You've met Miss Templar, Adela, haven't you?" he said turning to his stepmother.

A glimmer of recognition began to dawn in Mrs. Craig's cold blue eyes. She acknowledged Linden with the very slightest of frigid bows.

"Miss Templar is attending Paula," Randal explained briefly for the benefit of the rest of the party. "I'm glad to find you aren't always on call," he said to Linden, with a rather mocking look. "Let's hope your evening isn't interrupted by any untoward arrivals."

Linden managed a cool little smile and watched them move away. She saw Mrs. Craig look over her shoulder and murmur something to Randal. It was not difficult to guess what she was saying.

"Really, Randal, was that necessary? I'm sure you only embarrassed the girl. She looked quite out of her element as it was."

Mr. Templar was coming back from the telephone kiosk, and for an instant Linden was tempted to suggest that they should dine elsewhere. Then she realised that she had no adequate reason for the proposal, and anyway her father must be tired after the long drive and would not want to go out again even if she did have a good excuse. But her eager anticipation of their meal together was marred by the knowledge that Randal Craig might be watching her across the room.

The Craig party was already settled when they entered the restaurant and were ushered to a table. It was not until she had finished her shrimp cocktail that Linden allowed herself to glance towards them. Randal had his back to her, but at the very moment she looked at them, Melanie happened to be watching her, and Linden saw her murmur something to Mrs. Craig, who immediately stared icily at Linden and then at her father.

"Heavens! Can they possibly think that . . ." Linden remembered her laughing remark to her father earlier on and wondered if her lighthearted prophecy had come true. The idea that anyone could really misinterpret her relationship with her father was so outrageous that she could not help grinning. Of course she and Poppy weren't a bit alike, but even so the idea hardly seemed credible unless one was given to jumping to the most cynical conclusions on the flimsiest evidence.

The Craigs and their companions were still lingering over coffee when the Templars left the dining room.

"Oh, I almost forgot – I've got a parcel for you upstairs. Some of Louise's cast-offs," her father said suddenly.

"Oh, good! Anything exciting?" Linden asked eagerly.

Her sister was a designer for a leading wholesale dress manufacturer and was always superbly smart. She never wore anything for more than the season it was fashionable and usually passed her discarded garments on to Linden, whom they fitted with very little alteration.

"I've no idea. You'd better come up and investigate. If there's anything you don't want I'll take it back with me," said Mr. Templar.

They walked to the lift and waited for it to come down from the top floor. As the guide light above the gates flashed down to the second floor, Linden heard the dining room doors swish open and recognised Melanie's husky voice.

She did not look round and when the lift reached ground level and the grille slid open she stepped into the brightly lit compartment. "If they do suspect me of shady goings-on," she thought wickedly, "this will probably confirm their darkest doubts."

The next few days were uneventful and Linden spent most of her free time in making adjustments to the dresses that Louise had sent her. Some of them were not even out of fashion by London standards, and Linden suspected that Louise must have had another of the wholesale wardrobe purges to which she was periodically addicted. Perhaps she was embarking on another of her tempestuous love affairs and had felt the need to splurge on a completely new set of clothes.

Soon it was time for another visit to Paula Craig, who seemed in very good spirits now that the expected birth date was so near at hand. Linden left the house without meeting any of the other members of the family. This was better luck than she had anticipated, as she had been obliged to make the call about seven in the evening and had expected to disturb their evening meal.

She was approaching the turn of the drive and admiring the profusion of vivid scarlet flowers on the huge Britannia rhododendron which screened the bend, when a white sports car came sweeping round the turn in a flurry of flying gravel. It was travelling at such speed that, had she not been well to the left of the drive, Linden would not have stood a chance.

Instinctively, she wrenched the motor cycle on to the grass border. There was a terrifying screech of brakes and skidding tyres, and the next thing Linden knew was that she was lying in a heap on the grass with all the breath knocked out of her.

Dazed by the force of her fall, she lay blinking at the clear blue sky. Somewhere a door slammed and feet came thudding towards her. And then, as she tried to struggle up, a strong arm slid under her shoulders.

"Oh . . . hello," Linden said faintly.

Randal Craig's dark face was a mask of white-hot fury. "My God! She might have killed you!" he exclaimed furiously.

CHAPTER THREE

By this time, Linden had recovered sufficient breath to gasp, "The bike! Is the bike all right?"

"To the devil with that! Are *you* all right?" he demanded.

Linden moved her legs and then her arms. She was still breathing with difficulty, but otherwise she seemed to have survived intact.

"Yes, I'm fine," she said with relief. "If you could just give me your hand to stand up. I – I seem to have lost my hat. Oh, please, I don't need ..."

Her voice trailed off in astonishment as Randal picked her up in his arms and settled her against his chest.

"Now don't start fussing. We'll see to the bike presently. I want to make sure you haven't sprained anything," he said abruptly.

"But ... "

"Put your arm round my neck and hang on," he cut in sharply.

Since she was still too dizzy to be capable of argument, Linden did as she was told. Then, as they turned towards the house she saw the car. It was bonnet-deep in the bushes on the other side of the drive and Melanie Fletcher was leaning against the off-side looking pale and shaken.

"Is she hurt?" the other girl asked, as they came abreast of her. Her voice was ragged with fear and she looked as if she were about to faint.

"Apparently not," Randal answered, in a strange tone. As they neared the house, Linden became conscious of her disordered condition. Her skirt had ridden up above her knees, her tights were torn beyond repair and the pins had slipped out of her hair.

Randal carried her up the steps without any apparent effort and went to a small room on the right of the hall. Having laid her gently on a sofa with instructions not to move, he went swiftly across the room and opened a cupboard. A moment later he was back with a small tumbler.

"It's only brandy. Drink it!" he ordered crisply.

He must have pressed a bell as, a moment later, the maid appeared in the doorway and gave a startled squeak at the sight of Linden's dishevelment.

"It's all right, Mason. There's been an accident, but no one is seriously hurt. Fetch the first-aid box and one of Mrs. Andrew's dressing gowns, will you? If she's in her room, explain that Miss Templar has ripped her dress. We don't want her alarmed."

"And get me a stiff whisky, Mason," said Melanie, appearing in the doorway behind her. She was no longer white and frightened, but her hands trembled as she lit a cigarette.

"You'd better sit down in the drawing room, Melanie," said Randal, over his shoulder. He was kneeling by the sofa, unfastening Linden's shoes.

Melanie hesitated, gave Linden a hostile glance and then turned on her heel.

"I think I'd better ask the doctor to come and look you over," Randal said, frowning, as he dropped Linden's shoes on the floor.

"Oh, no!" Linden said vehemently. Then, in a calmer tone, "That really isn't necessary. I'd know if I'd broken any bones. If you could just phone the clinic and explain that I've had a slight accident."

"It was almost the end of your career," he said brusquely. "While I'm phoning, you'd better take your tights off. You've grazed both knees and there's a cut on your left ankle. I won't be long."

When he had gone, Linden peeled off her ruined tights and examined her injuries. Apart from minor abrasions and a battered sensation that would presently turn to stiffness, she felt surprisingly sound.

When Randal came back, she was examining the rent in her dress.

"Don't worry about that. I'll get Mason to stitch it up while you have a rest," he said. "I've spoken to Mrs. Langley at the clinic and she agrees that you shouldn't be called out tonight. I told her that the accident was entirely our fault."

The maid reappeared with a large metal box under one arm and a quilted housecoat over the other.

"Miss Fletcher seems ever so poorly, sir. Do you think she ought to lie down?" she asked.

"Ring up her home and ask them to fetch her, will you? She's only shaken up," Randal said briefly. "I'll need a bowl of warm water and some clean towels to attend to Miss Templar."

"Oh, please don't bother – I can easily mop myself up," Linden said awkwardly, attempting to sit up.

He pushed her gently but firmly back against the cushions. "You've had a bad shock. Just take it easy for a while."

It was a strange experience for Linden – being at the receiving end of medical attention. Randal was unexpectedly competent at dealing with her grazes. Or perhaps it was not so unexpected, she thought, as he carefully cleaned away the blood and grit. Whatever his other failings, he did not look the type to be floored by any emergency

"I wish you'd see if Miss Fletcher is all right," she said, as he finished his task. "It must be a horrible sensation – seeing somebody almost under your wheels."

He gave her a narrowed glance and ignored the suggestion. "I'll go and have a look at your bike. If it isn't too badly damaged, my garage should be able to fix it for you by tomorrow. Meanwhile you put on this dressing gown and I'll send Mason for your dress. You can't dash off till it's mended, so you'd better stay there and rest."

Before he left the room, he adjusted the venetian blinds so that the evening sunlight filtered through them in a soothing golden glow. The mellow half-light and the effect of the brandy made Linden feel quite drowsy and she was glad to close her eyes for a few minutes and relax against the soft cushions. A china clock ticked softly from somewhere behind her and there was a faint scent of roses on the air.

She must have dropped off for a moment. When she opened her eyes the light seemed dimmer and someone was talking in the hall.

"I can't see why you're making such a fuss!" Linden recognised the voice as Melanie's. "The fact is that she *isn't* seriously hurt. You don't seem at all worried about me."

"I've told you before that you drive like a maniac," Randal retorted impatiently.

There was a pause, and then Melanie said in a low, cajoling voice, "Oh, Randal, don't be so horrid to me. I've said I'm sorry."

Linden heard something that sounded like a muffled sob and then another longer silence.

"Suppose you apologise to her." This time Randal's voice was gentler although it still had an undertone of severity.

"Oh, Randal, for heaven's sake! She must know I didn't do the thing intentionally," Melanie said petulantly. "And it was really her own fault that she fell off at all. If she hadn't swerved on to the grass and if you hadn't grabbed the wheel, we'd all have been perfectly all right."

"If she wasn't a friend of ours, you'd probably be facing a charge of careless driving," Randal said sharply.

"It's certainly the last time I'll trust myself with you at the wheel, my girl."

"A friend of yours!" Linden could imagine the disdainful curve of Melanie's vivid lips. "I'm sure Adela doesn't regard her as a friend – particularly after what we saw at the Carlton the other night."

"What do you mean by that?"

"Oh, Randal, don't pretend to be naïve. Heaven knows where she managed to pick up such a presentable-looking man if she's only just arrived in the place, but it was perfectly obvious what was going on. Not that I mind what she does in her spare time – but I always thought that medical people had to be madly discreet."

"You must be off your head, Melanie. What possible grounds can you have for such a wild suggestion?" Randal said shortly.

"You needn't jump down my throat. Adela thought exactly the same. If it wasn't for upsetting Paula at the last moment, she was going to ask you to arrange for another nurse to attend her."

"Oh, she was, was she?" Randal said grimly.

By this time Linden was trying to find some way to let them know that the door had been left ajar. To cough would make it obvious that she had overheard the exchange. If only there was something she could drop!

But Melanie must have realised that her insinuations were not having the effect she intended as she suddenly changed tack and said in a softer voice, "Oh, don't let's quarrel about it, Randal. I've had about as much as I can take for one day."

The sound of a car coming up the drive muffled Randal's reply to this and by the time the motor was switched off, they appeared to have moved to the front door.

So much for the old saying that listeners seldom hear good of themselves, Linden reflected with a wry smile. She could only assume that Melanie's attempt to discredit her had been prompted by the older girl's fury at losing face before Randal. But for Linden's untimely appearance, that reckless piece of driving at the bend would probably have been dismissed with an indulgent remonstrance.

When Randal came back into the room, his expression gave no clue to his state of mind.

"Feeling better?" he asked pleasantly.

"Yes, much better, thank you. As soon as my dress is ready I'll be off your hands."

He picked up a silver box and handed it to her. "I know you smoke and you're not in uniform," he said, as she shook her head.

Linden smiled and changed her mind. As he held the lighter, she noticed again the lean shapeliness of his hands, and remembered how deftly he had used them to dress her cuts. In an uncharacteristic flight of fancy, she imagined him shaking back a Mechlin lace ruffle to flick open a snuff box or grip a duelling pistol.

Randal sat down on the other end of the sofa and crossed his long legs. "I've sent Miss Fletcher home. She wanted to apologise for giving you such a fright, but I thought you might be asleep," he said casually.

Linden looked politely expressionless. "It really doesn't matter. No permanent harm was done," she said mildly.

"The garage are sending up a truck for your motor cycle. Naturally we shall pay for the necessary repairs."

"Thank you."

There was a protracted silence while Randal watched his smoke drift slowly upwards and Linden tried desperately to think of something to say.

"I – I'm glad I'm not in London in this hot weather," she managed finally.

Randal turned his head and looked at her, his dark eyes glinting with laughter. "Are you, Nurse Templar?" he said quizzically.

She coloured, wishing the maid would hurry up and bring back her dress. It was a new and annoying sensation to be made self-conscious and nervy just by being alone with a comparative stranger. What was it about the man that was so unsettling? With Peter Carbury she would have been chatting and at ease. But the mere fact of Randal Craig's presence gave her much the same feeling as being in a room with a harmless but malevolent-looking spider. Except that Randal didn't look malevolent but might not be entirely harmless. She had an uncomfortable conviction that he knew his effect on her and was amused by it.

When brisk footsteps sounded in the hall, it took all her control not to let out a breath of relief. But it was not Mason but the senior Mrs. Craig who pushed open the door.

"Oh, there you are, Randal. What on earth is Melanie's car doing in the bushes on the drive? Has there been ..."

Randal had risen as she entered and now, briefly, he explained what had happened.

Mrs. Craig stopped short as she caught sight of Linden and her eyebrows arched.

His stepmother listened in silence, her eyes taking in Linden's bare legs and the borrowed dressing gown. Her mouth tightened.

"I see," she said slowly. "Well, surely Nurse would be better in her own home if she needs to rest."

"I shall take her home as soon as her dress is mended," Randal said evenly.

Mrs. Craig seemed about to speak, then changed her mind.

"I'd better telephone the Fletchers and find out if Melanie is all right," she said, after a pause. With a smile so forced as to be more like a grimace at Linden, she left the room.

It was not until Linden was dressed and he was

driving her home that Randal made an indirect reference to his stepmother's lack of cordiality.

"I'm afraid that, to some extent, you are the scapegoat for my misdoings, Miss Templar," he said suddenly.

He waited until they had passed a zebra crossing before going on. "I encouraged my sister-in-law to have her child at home, but unfortunately the plan doesn't meet with all-round approval."

"You may change your mind too, after it has arrived," Linden said dryly. "Even in a large house, a baby's howls can be amazingly penetrating."

He laughed. "I daresay we shall survive. You're one of a large family, aren't you?"

"Yes, I am. But what made you think so?"

He shrugged. "I just had that impression. Do you miss them?"

"I'm usually too busy to be homesick," she said lightly. "Of course we've all been out in the world for some time now. I think I should miss going home for Christmas. I've always been lucky so far, but I doubt if I shall be this year."

"That must be one if the main drawbacks of your work, isn't it? Having to work when other people are on holiday."

"Not really, because Christmas is a special day wherever you are. There's always plenty of Christmas spirit in hospital, and as far as midwifery is concerned, one shares with the family one's attending. It's the lonely old pensioners and the people who live by themselves that I feel sorry for at Christmas."

When they reached the flats, he handed her out of the car and took her case from the back seat.

"I'll carry it up for you," he said, as she held out her hand for it.

A shabby pram and a child's battered tricycle were parked outside the entrance to the block.

In the lower hall, several three-year-olds were happily stamping and shouting while a dribbling toddler sat on the lowest stair and played with an old kitchen strainer. Linden smiled to herself. On the Westleigh Estate, the presence of children was manifest a good deal more vigorously than was likely to be the case in Randal's household. Indeed, if his stepmother could impose her views, the Craig baby would probably only be visible for the shortest possible intervals when, in immaculate French lawn, it was brought down to the drawing room to be briefly admired by visitors.

Unlocking her front door, Linden tried to remember if she had had time to tidy the sitting room that morning. She had expected that Randal would put her case on a chair and leave at once. Instead, he followed her into the room and looked about him with frank interest.

Although, by comparision with the beautifully furnished apartments at the Craig house, the sitting room must appear very confined and commonplace, Linden had done everything possible to enliven its former bleakness. Gay cotton curtains and a plain pelmet framed the steel windows and a coral rug brightened the wood block floor. Perhaps the small Sheraton writing desk which came from her room at home was out of its element among the heavy moquette arm chairs and shiny oak table, and perhaps the Dufy print and her green glass swan – its broad back filled with white roses from the Carburys' garden – would have looked better above a fireplace less ugly than the Corporation fitting of mottled brown tiles, but these faults could not be helped. At least the books on the tightly packed shelves looked as if they had been read, unlike the rows of handsomely bound editions of classics which she had noticed in the room where she had rested.

"This is very pleasant. Who keeps it cleaned for you?" Randal asked, examining a Tretchikoff print of an arrangement of crimson poinsettias which she had hung on another wall.

"I do, of course," Linden said, amused.

His eyebrows went up. "You must be an early riser."

She pulled off her hat. Her hair was still loose, and catching sight of herself in the mirror, she saw that her lipstick needed retouching. The untidy hair and pale mouth above the stiffened white collar made her look like a schoolgirl.

"May I have a look?" Randal bent to inspect the bookshelves. "Freya Stark ... *The Rubaiyyat* ... A.A. Milne ... you have a catholic taste," he said with a quizzical look.

He picked out a book which Linden recognised as a collection of poems and began to skim through it.

As he showed no intention of leaving for the moment, Linden said, "I'm going to make some coffee. Would you like some?"

Randal put the book aside. "I'll help you." He must have seen the uncertainty of her expression, as he smiled and asked, "What's the matter? Is the kitchen in a shambles, or do you doubt my ability to be useful?"

Putting out the cups while Randal filled the percolator, Linden wondered what was his motive for this unexpected and rather disquieting show of friendliness. He was scarcely likely to be genuinely interested in the way she lived.

When the coffee was ready, he carried the tray into the sitting room and watched her pour it from the graceful Staffordshire pot. As long as the conversation kept on impersonal topics, Linden did not find it difficult to talk to him. They discussed summer holidays, and he was interested to learn that one year – in her training period – she had joined a party of students and helped to pick the grape harvest at a Burgundy vineyard near Rheims.

"Did you have to tread the grapes as well as pick them?" he asked.

"Oh, no – I think most of the growers have mechanical presses nowadays. But it was still a pretty hardworking holiday. We had to be up at dawn and pick until nearly sunset. After ten days of it, we were almost too tired to spend our earnings in Paris. I remember that getting back to the wards seemed like a rest cure for the first week or so."

"And this year?" he asked.

The ring of the doorbell prevented Linden from explaining that she had already had her holiday. She excused herself to answer it and found Jill Adams waiting outside.

"I heard you'd had a slight crack-up, so I popped round to see if you needed my help," Jill said, looking relieved by Linden's healthy appearance.

"Oh, that was nice of you, Jill. It wasn't anything serious. Come in."

Jill advanced into the room, caught sight of Randal and stopped short, an expression of comical astonishment on her pretty face.

"Oh...I didn't realise..." she began in embarrassment.

"This is Mr. Craig. Nurse Adams is one of my colleagues," Linden explained, as Randal rose to his feet.

Jill took his extended hand and managed a feeble smile. But her eyes were still wide with amazement and Linden saw a flicker of amusement at the corner of Randal's mouth.

When he had gone, after promising to let Linden have news of the motor cycle first thing in the morning, Jill was full of apologies.

"I say, I *am* sorry to have butted in!" she exclaimed anxiously. "Mrs. Langley said you'd had the accident

75

up at the Craigs', but I never dreamed that *he* would be here."

"It doesn't matter, Jill. He was just on the point of going before you arrived. What sort of day have you had?"

But Jill was not to be deflected from the more absorbing topic of Randal's presence in the flat.

"You seem to have made a hit," she said admiringly, having extracted the full details of the mishap.

"Oh, don't be silly," said Linden, with an uncomfortable laugh. "It was the least he could do to run me home. He was just being polite."

"I wouldn't mind having a crash if he was on hand to pick up the pieces," Jill said dreamily. Then, with a puzzled glance at Linden, who was running a comb through her hair, "Do you honestly mean you aren't in the least bit interested in him? Why, I think he's one of the most fabulously attractive men I've ever met. A real dreamboat!"

"I suppose he is quite nice-looking," Linden conceded without enthusiasm. "I can't see anything fabulous about him."

Jill stared at her incredulously. "Oh, come off it, Linden," she said, grinning. "I know there's not much future in it, but you might at least admit he's a terrific charmer. Haven't you noticed the way his left eyebrow shoots up and that gorgeous square chin with just the hint of a dent in it?"

"You certainly didn't miss much," Linden said, laughing. For one instant, when Jill had implied that she was only pretending to be uninterested in Randal, she had felt quite a strong flash of dislike for her friend. She had almost snapped back a cutting retort. Now she felt guilty and puzzled. Jill was only teasing: it was silly to take it in bad part.

"All the same, I'm not sure that I'd want to be married to a man like that. He's really more the type for a terrific *affair*, don't you think?" Jill said reflectively. Then seeing the twinkle in Linden's eyes, she added hastily, "Oh, I know he wouldn't give *me* a second glance – but he might you."

The idea of Jill engaging in a reckless love affair had restored Linden's good humour.

"Do you mean that I'm a more likely quarry for men with dishonourable intentions?" she asked gravely.

"Oh, no – of course I didn't," Jill said quickly. "But you might stand a chance against someone like the Fletcher girl, while I wouldn't have an earthly. You know, even in uniform, you have a sort of air about you, Linden."

Linden grinned. "I'd need more than an air to compete with wild mink jackets and dresses from Harrods' Model Room," she said dryly. "But what makes you think Mr. Craig isn't the marrying type?"

"I didn't say that," Jill corrected her. "I said I wouldn't want to be married to him. He isn't comfortable enough for someone like me. I want a husband who will potter in the garden on Sunday afternoon: someone homely and easy-going."

Linden picked up a rose petal that had fallen from the swan. The thought came to her that, if Randal Craig ever fell deeply in love with a woman, he was the type of man to adore her all his life. No, he wouldn't be a comfortable husband in the sense Jill meant the term. But neither would he be the dull, complacent, selfish kind of husband. He would never take his wife for granted, but neither would he allow her to take him for granted.

On the other hand, if he married someone like Melanie Fletcher, it would probably intensify that element of ruthlessness in him. Melanie might be able to make him love her, but Linden doubted if she was a woman who would ever give more than the most superficial kind of response to any man.

"What *are* you thinking about?" Jill asked. "You had the most ferocious expression on your face just then."

Linden dropped the petal in the waste basket. "Did I?" she said, lightly. "I – I was brooding over the ruin of my tights."

When Jill had gone, she made herself a Welsh rarebit and another pot of coffee. There was some washing to be ironed and a button missing from one of her blouses, but she felt disinclined to tackle either of these tasks and attributed her lethargy to delayed shock.

After a warm bath, she took two aspirins and went to bed. But although she had drawn the curtains to shut out the summer twilight, she could not sleep. Shifting restlessly about the narrow bed, she could hear the voices of the youths and girls at the corner of the street below her window. They were there every evening: the boys standing astride their shiny racing cycles, the girls sitting on the low brick wall in tight jeans, their curls bobbing as they chattered and giggled. Suddenly and absurdly, Linden envied them. To their teenage eyes, she probably looked quite old and staid: but surely twenty-four was too young to spend a warm summer night shut up in an airless bedroom. In London, there had always been someone who was throwing an impromptu coffee party or needing a fourth for some outing. Here, apart from Peter Carbury and her fellow nurses, she knew no one in her own age group. There was no chance of the telephone ringing, of some cheerful voice urging her to get up and dress and come and join a party.

In the flat below, someone turned on a radio and the lilt of beat music wafted upwards. Linden groaned and buried her head in the pillow. She did not analyse the reasons for her restless state of mind, and finally she drifted to sleep with the music still echoing in her dreams.

Next morning, apart from several bruises and a slight stiffness in one shoulder, Linden was none the worse for her misadventure. She was having breakfast in her housecoat when the door bell rang and she found a youth in oil-stained overalls waiting in the hall.

"Miss Templar? I've brought your motor cycle back, miss. Where'd you like me to put it?"

"Oh, is it repaired already?" she exclaimed, in surprise.

"Good as new, miss. I've left it on the road for the moment."

"It may as well stay there. I shall be going out presently. Was it very badly damaged?" Linden enquired.

"Nothing too bad." He detailed the extent of the damage which, to Linden, sounded quite extensive.

"Well, thank you very much for getting it done so quickly," she said gratefully.

"That's O.K., miss. If it gives you any trouble, just let us know. Mr. Craig said to make sure it was in good order and to charge it to his account."

The garage had carried out Randal's instructions so well that, when Linden went out some time later, she had to examine the cycle very closely to detect any signs of the accident. He must be one of their most important customers to exact such rapid and meticulous service, she thought with a faint smile.

Sandwiching a call at the butcher's shop between two visits to patients later in the morning, Linden met Mrs. Carbury coming out of a grocery shop. The older woman looked trim and capable in the neat uniform of the W.R.V.S. and was carrying a laden basket.

"I'm shopping for my pensioners," she said, with a smile, as they came abreast. "Hello! You look a bit in the wars."

Linden glanced down at the strips of adhesive dressing which showed through her tights, and explained what had happened.

"Oh, you're on the Craig case, are you?" Mrs.

Carbury said, looking interested. "How do you get on with Adela Craig? No, don't tell me. I'm sure it would be a breach of professional etiquette."

Linden laughed. It was clear that Mrs. Carbury did not care for the elder Mrs. Craig and took it for granted that Linden shared her dislike.

"Randal and Tom were at school together, you know," she went on, referring to her eldest son. "Randal came to tea once or twice. He was a strange little boy – very quiet and grave and with the most beautiful manners. I used to feel quite concerned about him until I discovered he was the ring-leader of several most hair-raising escapades. Then Tom went to the grammar school and Randal was sent away to Uppingham and they lost touch with each other."

They talked for a few more minutes and then Mrs. Carbury said she must dash away to her meals-on-wheels deliveries and hurried off, urging Linden to come up for supper again as soon as she had a free evening.

It was one of the hottest days of the year, and mid-afternoon found Linden waiting for the protracted arrival of the Barlow baby. Her shoulder seemed stiffer now and she longed for a cold drink and a respite from the stagnant heat of the cramped bedroom. On the other side of the bed, elderly Dr. Anderson mopped his glistening bald head and consulted his watch. Between them young Mrs. Barlow persevered gamely with the breathing technique which she had been taught at the clinic.

It was nearly eight o'clock when Linden left the house and stretched her aching back. Her dress clung damply to her waist and her temples ached with the heat and the prolonged effort of concentration.

Climbing the stairs to the flat, she was met by the occupant across the landing.

"This parcel came for you, Nurse. Special delivery.

I told the boy I couldn't say when you'd be back, so he asked me to take it in for you."

The parcel was thin and square, wrapped in the distinctive paper of one of the town's best shops. Puzzled, Linden looked at the address on the tag. It was typewritten and correctly addressed to her.

"Thank you, Mrs. Grant." She managed a wan smile, her whole body aching for the refreshment of a cold bath and clean clothes.

"I say, you look properly worn out, dear," Mrs. Grant said sympathetically. "Been on a difficult case?" Without waiting for Linden to reply, she crossed her muscular arms, leaned comfortably against the landing wall and, in a tone of morbid relish, began to recount the details of her own confinements.

Linden repressed her irritation and waited for a chance to cut it, but it was ten minutes before she could make her escape without offending her garrulous neighbour.

"I've a pot of tea on the stove if you'd like a cup," Mrs. Grant called after her, as she unlocked her door.

"Thanks, but I haven't too much time." Linden ducked quickly inside the door and leaned her back against it with a breath of relief.

It was not until she had bathed and changed that she opened the mysterious parcel. Inside the scarlet and gold box of a noted hosiery firm were three pairs of sheer grey tights. They were of much finer quality than Linden usually wore for work, but they were the right size. There was no card with them.

Perhaps she was being unfairly captious, but as she put the box away, Linden reflected that she would have much preferred a brief note of sincere apology to the expensive replacement of her tights. Yet it was just the kind of gesture which one would expect of Melanie Fletcher. A telephoned order to the store . . . instructions for the parcel to be delivered at once and charged to account . . . and that was an end of the whole aggravating episode.

While she was waiting for her cutlets to grill, Linden wrote a short note to thank Melanie for the tights. Then she looked up the Fletchers' address in the telephone directory and also Randal's number.

It was the senior Mrs. Craig who answered the call. Hoping her voice would not be recognised, Linden asked for Randal.

"Who is that speaking, please?"

Linden was obliged to give her name.

"I'll see if he is in, Nurse." There was a silence for several minutes, then the sound of the receiver being picked up. "I am sorry, Mr. Craig is not in."

"Oh . . . well, would you tell him the motor cycle is running perfectly and thank him for me, please?"

"Certainly. Goodbye." Almost before Linden had time to answer, the other receiver clicked back on its rest.

Linden had intended to go home on her first long weekend, but when the time came the weather was still so hot she could not face the train journey and the stifling humidity of the city. Melchester was only thirty miles from the sea, so on the Friday morning she rose early and drove to the coast and spent a long day lazing on the beach. The expedition would have been more fun with a companion but nevertheless she enjoyed herself and came back browned and invigorated by the fresh salt breeze.

On Saturday morning, Mrs. Carbury rang up to ask if she would come to an informal party and, with her evening planned, Linden spent the morning shopping and the afternoon getting ready. At seven o'clock, with her hair freshly washed and her face carefully made up with a new coral lipstick and a touch of silver-green eye shadow, she ran downstairs. Her dress – one of those which her sister had sent her – was a sophisticated version of a school gym tunic, made of fluid ivory silk and belted with narrow gold kid. Before leaving the flat, Linden had experimented with several changes of jewellery and finally decided that it looked best without any ornament.

"My dear, you do look nice!" her hostess greeted her warmly, when she arrived. "Come and be introduced. Poor Peter has just been called out, but I expect he'll be back for supper."

It was nearly nine o'clock when Peter returned. Linden thought he looked tired and strained and suspected that it was an effort for him to be sociable. But when he saw her, he smiled and came quickly across to where she was sitting.

"Hello there! I heard you were on a long weekend and asked Mother to call you, but I thought you might have gone home."

"I couldn't face London in this heatwave," she said smiling.

"Good." He sat down beside her and something in his glance made her suddenly shy.

"What have you been doing?" she asked.

He frowned. "Waiting for a poor old boy to die. There was nothing I could do except be there. If Mother asks me about it, try to head her off, will you? He was one of the pensioners she visits. I don't want her evening spoiled."

"No, of course not. I'm so sorry," Linden said gently.

He shrugged. "I should be used to it by now – but it's a bit miserable when people have no one of their own to be with them."

"You must be tired. I expect you're wishing us all at the bottom of the sea," Linden said sympathetically.

His expression lightened. "The others, perhaps. Who's taking you home – or may I?"

"I shouldn't dream of dragging you out again," she said firmly. "Anyway I've got my steed with me."

"And nothing to put over that dress, I suppose? You'll catch a chill, riding with bare shoulders. I'll run you home and you can pick up the bike tomorrow. You're coming on this picnic, aren't you?"

"I don't know anything about it," Linden said questioningly.

"I expect Mother's forgotten to mention it. We're taking a packed lunch to our chalet at Northbeach. It's one of the few places that aren't jammed with cars at the weekend. I think you'll like it."

"It sounds lovely, but ..." Linden said uncertainly.

"Fine, that's settled, then. I'll bring the bike round about ten and Mother will follow in the car. We're taking a couple of kids with us, so be prepared for a bit of a crush."

The party broke up about eleven and, when the other guests had gone, Peter tucked Linden into his car.

"Better drape this round you," he said, producing a thick sweater from the back seat.

The heat of the day still lingered in the still night air, and it was refreshing to feel a current of coolness brushing her face and neck as they gathered speed. Pleasantly drowsy, Linden relaxed in her seat and half closed her eyes. It was not until she judged that they were nearly there that she roused herself and realized that they were on the outskirts of the town and well away from the estate.

"I thought you might like a quiet spin for half an hour before turning in," Peter said, glancing at her.

"But aren't you longing for bed? she said doubtfully.

"It's too hot to sleep yet."

They drove in silence for a while, passing the last scattered houses and coming to fields and woods, the headlights probing the hedges as the road became more winding. At last, at the top of a long incline, Peter eased off the accelerator and turned the car on to a stretch of common land.

"There you are! An owl's eye view of Melchester."

Seen from this height and distance, the town looked smaller and more compact. There was a curious remoteness about that haze of different coloured lights. It was like being in an aeroplane and flying over some unknown, unnamed city and wondering about all those people below, or passing by in a train and glimpsing a child's night-light or the weird bluish glow of a television screen. It made one feel curiously lonely and a little afraid.

She must have given an involuntary shiver, as Peter touched her arm. "Feeling chilly now?" he asked quickly.

She shook her head. Now that the headlights were out, her eyes were becoming accustomed to the moonlight and she could see him quite clearly.

His fingers still resting lightly on her arm, Peter said quietly, "I suppose that, according to the book, this outing is rather irregular. Not that anyone we know is likely to be lurking in the bushes, but it's astonishing how quickly the tongues start to wag if a doctor and nurse are seen together in anything but strictly professional circumstances."

"It must be more difficult to tell someone off if you know them socially," Linden said casually.

"Do you think it's likely that I shall have to tell you off some time?" he asked, sounding amused.

"You might," she said evenly.

He began to fill his pipe, "At moments like this I find it very hard to realize that you are a nurse. That's a very attractive get-up."

Linden smiled to herself at the thought of her sister's reaction to such a compliment. Anyone who described a dress of Louise's as a "get-up" would get a very chilly glance in return. In fact Louise would not approve of

Peter at all. "Oh, darling! not *another* of those overgrown schoolboys!" she would protest. But then all she would notice about Peter was his untidy hair and lack of urbanity.

"You make it sound as if we were all the most dreary frumps. That's not fair," she objected mildly. "It isn't our fault that we have to wear rather dull uniforms most of the time."

"On the contrary, I think the uniform is very becoming," he said seriously. "There's something about the rustle of starch and a neat pair of black-stockinged ankles that a girl in ordinary clothes hasn't got."

Linden laughed. "Shades of the can-can, perhaps," she answered teasingly.

A few minutes later, he started the car and took her home. But, although she had enjoyed the short drive, Linden got ready for bed in a rather troubled mood. She had a feeling that her friendship with Peter was progressing too rapidly and that this was unwise, both for professional and personal reasons. She almost wished that she had not agreed to go on the picnic tomorrow.

Next morning, Linden hurried to the sweet shop and bought some chocolate wafers and potato crisps. She had no doubt that Mrs. Carbury would provide an ample lunch basket, but on any expedition that included children, extra supplies were always welcome.

She was waiting on the edge of the curb when Peter arrived on her motor bike with the car following behind. While he was putting the bike in the courtyard behind the flats, Linden was introduced to the two children, Bobby aged nine, and Suzy, his seven-year-old sister. Their parents had gone abroad for ten days and the youngsters were staying with Mrs. Carbury until they returned.

They reached the coast soon after eleven and the children tore off their shirts and shorts and rushed down to the water with Peter following to keep an eye on them. Linden helped Mrs. Carbury to arrange their baggage in the shade of a canvas windbreak and to set up the three deckchairs.

There were a few other families on the beach, but having no tea stalls or ice-cream kiosks, it was less popular than the more commercialised bathing places and never overcrowded, said Mrs. Carbury.

"Don't feel you must stay with me, dear. I expect you're longing for a dip," she added, as Linden wriggled out of her cotton jeans.

"I think I'll bask for a while. What a heavenly day!" Linden said, searching for her sunglasses.

"Poor Peter! I think they're trying to drown him." Constance Carbury shaded her eyes with her hand to watch the group in the water. There was silence for some minutes, and then she said suddenly, "My husband and I were planning to live here when he retired, but I think I should find it too lonely in the winter by myself. When Peter marries I shall probably join my sister in the south. She's a school-mistress and has a very nice house near Brighton. I could carry on with my W.R.V.S. work, but have time to go up to London and see all the shows."

"But wouldn't you miss Melchester?" Linden asked.

"I don't think so. It's never been quite the same for me since John died. I only stayed for Peter's benefit because it's so difficult to get a good housekeeper. Once he has a wife to look after him, I can lead my own life again. And mothers-in-law are much more popular when they keep at a reasonable distance, you know."

"I should think you would make an ideal mother-in-law," Linden said impulsively. "It's bound to be terribly difficult to give up one's son to some hare-brained girl who can hardly boil an egg and forgets to darn his socks."

"Perhaps – if one tends to be possessive by nature,"

Mrs. Carbury agreed. "I've always tried to avoid that. I think being happy with one's husband has a great deal to do with it. John and I were very happy together and – much as we loved them – the boys took second place."

"Yes, my parents are like that," Linden said thoughtfully. "They love having us with them, but now that we're all grown-up, they're perfectly content with each other."

The children came pelting up the beach like a couple of boisterous terriers.

"Aren't you going to bathe, Linden? It's lovely and warm," Bobby promised her.

Soon it was time for lunch, and then the children wanted to explore the distant headland. They raced ahead while Peter and Linden followed more leisurely.

"This is bliss! Much better than sweltering in London," Linden said happily, as they strolled along the tide-line.

Peter made her put her shirt over her bathing suit because the sun was at its height now, although a light breeze saved the brilliance from being uncomfortable.

"You look about twelve years old," he said, smiling at her as she paddled through the tepid shallows.

The children were far ahead, bending over some treasure they had found.

"Oh, look! A bottle! Perhaps there's a message in it." She waded out to knee-depth and grabbed the bobbing bottle. But it was only an empty gin bottle with a rotting cork.

"Look out! There's a jellyfish floating towards you." Peter took her wrist to draw her out of the way.

Linden turned, trod on something sharp and lost her balance. He caught her round the waist and steadied her.

"Cut yourself?"

They were very close. Instinctively, she had grasped

his shoulder to balance herself. His skin was warm and smooth beneath her wet palm and she could feel the hardness of muscle against her forearm.

"No, I – I don't think so."

His hold tightened. "Linden . . ." he said huskily. Then she was pulled hard against him and he was kissing her.

"Coo – ee! Uncle Peter!" The children were racing back towards them.

Peter let her go, and looked along the beach. He was breathing rather hard and his hands were clenched.

"Look what we've found!" The children splashed breathlessly towards them.

"He is a whopper, isn't he?" Peter examined the large crab which Bobby had trapped in his sister's bucket. "Look, Linden's hurt her foot. I'd better have a look at it."

The four of them moved up to the dry sand and Linden sat down.

"Are you bleeding?" Bobby asked hopefully.

She smiled at him, still too startled by the swiftness of what had happened to know what she felt. Peter knelt and examined the sole of her right foot. His hands were quite steady, but there was a pulse beating at his temple.

"No, it isn't cut after all," he said quietly.

"One of the chaps at school found a dead body in the sea last year," said Bobby, with macabre relish. "It must have been in for ages because he said it was . . ."

Linden saw Suzy casting an alarmed glance at the water. "What are you going to do with your crab?" she asked quickly.

Bobby had plans for starting an aquarium, but was finally persuaded that the crab would be happier in its native surroundings. Then Suzy announced that she was thirsty, so they returned to Mrs. Carbury.

All afternoon, Linden was conscious that Peter was

waiting for an opportunity to speak to her privately. To her relief, the children stayed close. She knew that eventually she must face him, but at present her thoughts were too confused for her to decide how to meet the situation.

With anyone else, she would have taken for granted that the kiss was no more than a passing impulse born of the bright summer day and an uncomplicated attraction. But, because of their professional connection, any attraction between them *was* complicated, and Peter must see that as clearly as she did.

Examining her reaction to the kiss after an interval which should have made it possible to do this with some detachment, she found it hard to determine what her feelings had been. Certainly she had not disliked it; but then no normal girl could object to being kissed by a good-looking young man for whom she already felt friendship. On the other hand, she had not experienced any startlingly strong response – no flurried beating of the heart, no breathless delight.

Catching Mrs. Carbury watching her, Linden shifted uncomfortably. Had his mother seen them embracing? For the first time she read a deeper significance of Constance Carbury's remarks about what she would do when Peter married.

Oh, this is absurd! I've only known him a few weeks, she thought impatiently. But, on the drive home, she found it hard to sound casual and lighthearted and was preoccupied with thinking of an adequate excuse if Mrs. Carbury suggested that she should spend the evening with them.

"You'll have supper with us won't you, Linden?" the older woman said, as they entered the outskirts of Melchester.

"That's very kind of you, but I promised to see Nurse Adams this evening," Linden said guiltily. "I have enjoyed today."

Peter dropped her at the flat without comment, and she was able to forestall him from seeing her to the door. Standing on the pavement, waving them on their way, she wondered if she had been mistaken, and that he, too, wanted a breathing space before they met again.

On Monday the weather broke. It was still warm, but there were showers all morning and thunder rumbling in the distance. By lunch time, the sky was completely overcast, and Linden – whose break did not end till midnight – spent the afternoon at the cinema. When she came out, the rain was driving down and she was glad she had carried her raincoat.

The evening was occupied with housework and making a rabbit casserole for Tuesday's lunch. Right up to ten o'clock she was unconsciously tensed for the telephone to ring or to hear a rap at the door and find Peter standing outside.

Jill had had a busy weekend, but Tuesday and Wednesday were quiet and Linden did not expect any of her patients to call her much before Friday. But on Wednesday night the insistent note of the telephone roused her from sleep.

Switching on the lamp, she looked at her watch. It was half-past one.

"Nurse Templar speaking." Her voice was husky from sleep.

"This is Randal Craig. Can you come over immediately? Paula's had an accident."

Linden sat upright with a jerk and pushed back the covers.

"What's happened?" she asked sharply, reaching for her clothes.

"She fell on the stairs. She doesn't seem to have hurt herself, but she thinks it has started the baby."

"Keep her warm and don't let her get in a panic. I'll be there in fifteen minutes." Linden snapped down the receiver, and began to tug on her clothes.

CHAPTER FOUR

RANDAL must have heard the motor cycle coming up the drive as he opened the door before she could press the bell. He was wearing a dark silk dressing gown over grey pyjamas and his hair was rumpled, but his manner was calm and practical.

"Good girl! You must have been jet-propelled," he said, with a shade of humour as they went towards the stairs.

"I'm used to dressing in a hurry," Linden said briefly. "How is she?"

"She seems more excited than anything, but it's unfortunate this should happen while Andrew's away."

"Away?" Linden queried.

"Yes, he had to go up to town today and phoned us earlier to say he'd decided to stop overnight."

They had reached the landing, and as they went towards Paula's bedroom, another door opened and Mrs. Craig appeared. She was fastening an elaborate quilted robe and her hair was concealed by a bandeau of ruched chiffon. Without make-up and with a film of night cream on her skin, she looked older and more haggard.

"What *is* going on?" she demanded. Then, seeing Linden, "What has happened? Why wasn't I called?"

"Paula thinks the baby may be arriving, Adela," Randal said coolly.

"Have you sent for the doctor?"

"I thought Nurse Templar would be the best judge of whether that was necessary yet," Randal replied.

Mrs. Craig flashed him an angry glance. "Really, Randal, I think you might have consulted ..."

Linden heard a low sound from the other room. "I'll go in," she said quickly. Then as Mrs. Craig made to accompany her, "I think I had better see her alone for the moment."

Paula was lying on top of the bed with a blanket draped over her legs. She gave a long sigh of relief when she saw Linden.

"Hello. I am sorry to get you out at this hour," she said shakily. "It was silly of me to . . . ooh!" She drew in a sharp breath and her hands clenched on the blanket.

Linden sat down on the bed and waited until the girl had relaxed again.

"Now, what's all this about falling downstairs?" she asked cheerfully.

Paula licked her lips. "I – I couldn't sleep, so I went down to make some tea. I must have tripped on my dressing gown. Luckily Randal was awake too. He heard me fall and carried me back to bed."

"So you never got that tea," Linden said smiling. She felt Paula's pulse. "Would you like some now?"

"Oh, yes, please. Nurse . . . you don't think my falling will have hurt the baby, do you?"

"Of course not. It may have hurried it up a bit, but they're tough little creatures," Linden assured her. "Look, you sit tight for a minute and I'll get your tea organised."

On the landing Mrs. Craig was pacing impatiently about while Randal stood looking down the stairs and drawing on a cigarette.

"Well?" Mrs. Craig demanded, as Linden came out of the bedroom.

"I don't think we'll need the doctor yet," Linden said quietly. She turned to Randal. "Would you fetch the gas and air machine from my carrier, please? Leave it out here for the moment. Oh – and could you make some tea?"

"Of course." Randal turned and went down the stairs.

"You might as well go back to bed, Mrs. Craig," Linden said casually. "I think the baby is definitely on the way, but it may be some hours before there's any important progress."

"Back to bed!" Mrs. Craig looked outraged at the suggestion. "I shouldn't dream of going back to bed, Nurse. I want to see my daughter-in-law."

"Very well – but only for a few minutes, please. She needs to rest while she can," Linden said mildly.

Mrs. Craig swept into the bedroom. "You should have called me immediately, Paula," she said peremptorily. "I can't imagine why you woke Randal."

Since Randal had evidently not told his step-mother about the accident, Linden hoped that Paula would not refer to it. This was not the moment for her to be lectured for carelessness. Wisely, Paula said nothing.

"How do you feel?" her mother-in-law enquired.

For answer, Paula clutched the blanket again and cast a beseeching glance at Linden.

"I really think we should call the doctor at once, Nurse," Mrs. Craig said sharply.

Linden ignored her until until her patient was resting again.

Then, evenly but with a note of authority, she said, "You needn't worry, Mrs. Craig. I shall call Dr. Henderson as soon as it's necessary. There's nothing he can do at present. Now, if you don't mind, I'd like to start my preparations."

For a moment she thought that Adela Craig was going to refuse to leave. Then, with a glacial stare and tightened lips, the older woman stalked angrily out.

"Oh dear, I'm sure she's furious. But I really don't want an audience," Paula said worriedly. "I wish Andrew was here."

"Never mind. You'll be able to surprise him,"

Linden said encouragingly, and snapped her case open.

Presently there was a tap on the door and Linden found Randal waiting with a tray of tea things. "Anything else I can do?" he asked.

"Is that Randal?" said Paula. "Can I see him for a minute?"

Randal cocked an eyebrow and Linden nodded. He carried the tray to the bedside table and smiled down at Paula. "Feeling better?" he asked gently.

She nodded. "Yes, much better. Look, Randal, can you keep Adela out of the way for a bit? I know she means to be kind, but she fidgets me."

"Of course. I'm just going to ring Andrew and tell him the good news. He can be here in a couple of hours with the roads clear."

"Oh, no, don't," Paula said quickly. "He'll only worry about me all the way, and I want him to walk in tomorrow and find the baby here. Please, Randal!"

He glanced doubtfully at Linden. "I think he ought to be told, Paula," he said quietly.

"But why? Nothing is going to go wrong, is it, Nurse?" Paula appealed to her.

"Of course not," Linden said, smiling. "But your husband might be annoyed if no one told him, and he'll certainly have an easier trip if he starts tonight when there's hardly any traffic. You may still be able to surprise him if the baby gets a move on."

"Oh, all right," Paula said reluctantly. "But do make him promise to drive carefully, Randal."

Randal nodded and gave her an encouraging pat on the shoulder. "I'll leave you to do your stuff," he said, with a grin. "I'll be in my room along the landing if you want me, Nurse."

It was six o'clock and the first pale glimmer of dawn was lightening the horizon when Linden heard the doctor's car pull up on the gravel below. An hour later, the baby gave its first plaintive cry.

"There you are, m'dear. What do you think of your daughter?" Dr. Henderson said cheerfully.

Paula gazed at the infant's resentful purple face. "She's lovely!" she said softly. "Oh, thank you so much."

"Don't thank me. Nurse Templar's done all the work," the doctor said, chuckling. "I might just as well have stayed in bed. Shall I go and announce the good news?"

The curtains were drawn back and sunlight was streaming into the room when Linden took off her white mask and gown. Andrew Craig had arrived a few minutes after the baby and was sitting by his wife's side. The doctor had left long ago and Adela Craig had been in to inspect her granddaughter, but Randal had not yet appeared.

"I think it might be a good idea for you to have a nap, Mrs. Craig," said Linden, pulling on her hat.

"Oh, I feel *much* too excited to sleep," Paula exclaimed happily.

"All the same, you need lots of rest, darling," Andrew said solicitously.

"You too, Mr. Craig. You may be up all night again if the baby starts howling," Linden said laughingly. "I'll leave you now, but I'll look in this afternoon. You make your wife go to sleep, Mr. Craig."

Smiling at their profuse thanks for her services, she picked up her bag and left them.

As she turned the bend of the stairs, she found Randal standing in the hall.

"Good morning. You can have a peep at your niece if you don't stay too long," she said, as he looked up and saw her.

"I'll look in later. Come in here a moment." He took her bag, put it on a hall chair and propelled her towards the room where she had rested on her last visit to the house.

96

This morning the blinds were drawn and the room was bright with sunshine. In the bay of the window a table was laid for breakfast. There was the fragance of freshly-ground coffee in the air.

"You need a good breakfast after working half the night," Randal said firmly, drawing out a chair for her. He moved away to press a bell. "I asked for bacon and eggs. Is that all right?"

"It sounds wonderful," Linden said, suddenly discovering that she was keenly hungry.

Randal sat down in the opposite chair and poured out two cups of coffee. "I had mine earlier. Do you mind if I smoke?" he asked.

She shook her head, wondering if he too had been up all night. He gave no sign of tiredness.

"What happens now?" he asked. "Do you get the rest of the day off?"

Linden sipped the coffee appreciatively. "No, I'll probably have a couple of hours' sleep and then I've got some calls. I'll be back to see your sister-in-law this afternoon," she explained.

"You must be a good deal tougher than you look," he said dryly.

"Do I look so frail?" she asked, smiling.

"Frail enough to need reasonable hours of sleep."

"I get them – but at different times from most people."

The maid came in with covered dishes on a tray. Randal watched Linden eat the crisp rashers of bacon and lightly poached eggs, but she was too hungry to mind his regard.

"Why did you dislike me so much for the first couple of weeks?" he said suddenly.

Linden gave him a startled glance. "I – I think you must have imagined it," she said evasively. "Why should I dislike you?"

97

His smile was sardonic. "For any number of reasons, I should think. More coffee?"

"Please." She made a complication of buttering a piece of toast. "Perhaps your attitude in the train annoyed me," she said coolly.

"Oh, yes, the fateful journey," he said quizzically. "What's become of your impassioned young suitor?"

"I don't know," Linden said shortly.

"That seems a rather callous attitude. He looked pretty far gone to me."

"Yes, I'm sure you didn't miss anything," Linden said sweetly.

Randal laughed. "Is that really why you gave me such a very cold shoulder – because I saw him kissing you goodbye?"

For a moment she was tempted to tell him the real reason – that gallingly derisive remark he had made to Melanie Fletcher.

"Perhaps you'd have been equally annoyed if I'd goggled at your farewells," she said, trying to sound flippant.

"Unfortunately for me, I've never been seized at the eleventh hour," he said with a mocking look.

Linden laid the thick damask napkin by her plate. "Thank you very much for the breakfast, Mr. Craig. I must go now," she said politely.

He went with her to the door. The gas and air apparatus was already strapped to her carrier and he fixed her bag in place.

"By the way, how is it running? Any trouble?" he asked.

"No, it's perfect, I did phone to thank you, but you were out."

"Oh? Mason didn't mention it."

She almost corrected him, then stopped. Perhaps Mrs. Craig had forgotten to relay her message. Or had she deliberately ignored it?

"Anyway, thank you for having it fixed. I hope it wasn't too ruinous," she said quickly.

"We owe you a great deal more than that," he said quietly, holding out his hand.

As his fingers closed firmly over hers, Linden wondered how anyone could be so maddening most of the time and then, unexpectedly, so nice.

That night Peter rang up. He wanted to take her for a drive.

"Oh, Peter, I can't. I was up all last night with the Craig baby. I must get to bed early," Linden explained.

"It's only half-past nine. A run out for half an hour would do you good."

"No, I can't possibly. I have to wash my hair and do a hundred other things. Another night, perhaps."

There was a pause until he said in a low voice, "Are you trying to avoid me, Linden?"

"What a peculiar idea," she said, trying to sound casual.

There was a sound like a stifled expletive at the other end of the line. Then he said, "I'll ring you later in the week, then."

"Yes, do. Goodnight, Peter." Linden replaced the receiver with a troubled frown.

She was unable to call at the Craig house on Friday as she was busy at another confinement. But on Saturday she arrived to find Paula in excellent spirits and wanting to get up.

"Not until Dr. Henderson says you may," Linden said firmly.

She had prepared the baby's bath – carrying it into the bedroom so that Paula could watch the procedure – when there was a knock at the door and Randal looked in.

"Oh, come in, Randal. You're just in time to see Jennifer being tubbed," Paula said eagerly.

"Do you mind if I stay?" he asked Linden.

"Not at all," she said politely.

Randal pulled up a chair and sat down. He was wearing a casual shirt and jeans. Presumably he did not go to his office on Saturdays.

Linden took off her wrist watch and began to undress the infant. It was beginning to rouse from the torpor of the first few days and stared hazily up at her, its tiny fist waving aimlessly.

Linden had lost count of the number of times she had bathed a slippery infant, but this morning some of her practised competence seemed to have deserted her. She knew this was because Randal was watching and was impatient with herself for being so easily discomposed.

"She's still very purple. Is that all right, Nurse?" Paula asked anxiously.

Linden laughed and reassured her. As she fastened the tiny jacket, the baby began to cry. For so small a creature, it had a lusty yell.

"Would you like to hold her for a moment, Mr. Craig?" Linden asked blandly, depositing the baby in his arms before he had time to protest.

But if she had hoped to see him look alarmed, she was disappointed. Randal accepted the infant without demur, propped it comfortably against his broad shoulder and began to pat its back.

"Oh, Randal, you'll hurt her!" Paula exclaimed in alarm. "Do mind her poor little head."

The baby gave a couple of resounding burps, widened its eyes in surprise and then slumped contentedly into a doze. Over its downy head, Randal gave Linden a long amused look.

"You seem to be quite an expert, Mr. Craig," she said evenly, retrieving his somnolent niece. "Oh dear! I'm afraid she's dribbled on you."

With a satisfaction that she knew to be childish, she

watched him produce a handkerchief and wipe the immaculate shirt.

"It serves him right for being so smug," Paula said, echoing her thoughts. "If you're as expert as all that, Randal, you can take your turn at two o'clock in the morning. Poor Andrew was patting her for hours last night."

There was another tap at the door and the maid appeared.

"Miss Fletcher has called, Mrs. Andrew. Shall I bring her up?"

Paula looked enquiringly at Linden. "I can see her, can't I? I'm not a bit tired."

"Yes, just for a little while. But it will soon be time for Jennifer's feed."

Paula seized her hand mirror and quickly applied fresh lipstick. "I don't want to look too maternal," she said with a laugh.

Melanie came into the room in an aura of expensive scent. She was wearing a black linen sheath dress with a mimosa scarf and matching linen shoes.

"Darling! How lovely to see you again! How are you?" she exclaimed, bending to kiss Paula's cheek and laying a large florist's sheaf and a long white box on the bed.

"I feel wonderful. Mm . . . what heavenly carnations! How nice of you," Paula said warmly, admiring the pink and white blooms. She undid the silver ribbons on the box and lifted the lid. Inside, swathed in palest rose tissue, was an exquisitely fine Shetland shawl, as soft as a drift of snowflakes. "Oh, Melanie, it's beautiful! Thank you!" she said delightedly.

"What do you think of Jennifer?" Randal asked.

Melanie turned to him, smiling. "Hello, Randal," she said softly. Then she looked at Linden and the baby. "Good morning, Nurse."

"Good morning." Linden turned to Paula. "If you'll

take Jennifer, I'll clear her bath things away, Mrs. Craig."

"Can I empty this for you?" Randal lifted the primrose plastic bath from its stand and waited for her to precede him into the adjoining room.

He tipped the soapy water into the hand-basin and stood aside while Linden wiped the bath and put it away in a cupboard.

"Are you on duty all day?" he said.

Linden nodded and moved past him to put the bath towels in the electric drying cabinet.

"You're bristling again," he said teasingly. "I thought we'd declared a truce. Or are you annoyed because I didn't flinch when you dumped the infant on me?"

She opened her mouth to deny it, stopped short and gave an unwilling laugh. "Does anything put you out of countenance, Mr. Craig?" she asked wryly.

"Occasionally." He watched her fill in the record sheet and replace it on a shelf with her overall. "Can we offer you some coffee before you leave?"

"Thank you, but I must get on now." She glanced at her watch. "I have two more calls before lunch."

In the bedroom, Melanie was sitting on the end of the bed, her skirt outlining shapely knees, the sunlight burnishing her lustrous coppery hair.

She rose as they entered. "I'd better go now, darling. I mustn't tire you. The baby's too sweet!" She touched the infant's cheek with a slender crimson-tipped finger, her smile tender.

Very touching! Linden thought coldly. Let's hope Randal is impressed.

As they left the room, she was shocked by the strength of her hostile feelings towards the other girl.

When, later that day, Linden was called to attend Mrs. Howlett, she knew she would have to face Peter again.

Jane Howlett was something of a problem case. She was only nineteen and had made it very clear that she resented the coming baby, and the consequent restriction of her social life. She had refused to attend either the talks or the relaxation classes at the clinic, and Linden suspected that she had not taken the extra milk and vitamins to which she was entitled. When Linden had visited her – and it had usually involved calling several times to catch her at home – she had been either sullen or bored, resisting all attempts to rouse her interest.

The door was opened by a big curly-haired man in mechanic's overalls. He looked harassed and nervous and was clearly immensely relieved by Linden's arrival.

"She's upstairs, Nurse. I wanted to call you sooner, but she wouldn't let me," he said anxiously.

The house was in its usual state of untidiness and neglect, and Linden wondered if her patient had bothered to make any of the necessary preparations. If not – and labour was already well advanced – it was going to be a trying evening.

She found Jane crouched on the bed with wide terrified eyes and trembling lips. When she saw Linden the girl attempted to assume her usual sulky detachment but her fear was too urgent to be masked.

"Shall I call the doctor, Nurse?" her husband asked, through the half-closed door.

Jane's hand fastened convulsively on Linden's arm. "Don't let him in," she whispered hoarsely. "Swear you won't let him in. I don't want him to see me."

Linden disengaged her arm and went to the door. "Yes, I think I had better phone him, Mr. Howlett," she said quietly. "Put a kettle on before you go, will you?"

By the time Peter arrived, Linden had put the bedroom in order and made up the baby's cot. Jane had directed her to open a suitcase concealed in the tiny box-room, and Linden had been surprised to find a complete layette of woolly garments which were now airing by the fire.

Presently, coming downstairs for a jug, Linden found Tom Howlett fingering a tiny vest with a puzzled expression.

"I didn't know she had all this stuff," he said, half to himself. Then, looking up, "She'll be all right, Nurse, won't she?"

Linden reassured him, and thought of several small tasks to keep him occupied. Jane Howlett's strange behaviour was becoming even more of a puzzle.

The child was born at midnight, already the image of its father with strongly marked eyebrows and a fine crop of dark curls plastered to its head. Linden wrapped him in a soft towel and laid him gently by his mother. For an instant an expression of intense delight and pride illumined the girl's wan face, but, almost immediately, she turned her head away and looked stonily at the wall. Across the bed, Peter raised enquiring eyebrows. Linden made a small gesture of bewilderment.

When she went downstairs she found Tom Howlett gnawing his knuckles at the kitchen table, a saucerful of half-smoked cigarette stubs at his elbow.

He sprang to his feet. "Is she . . .?"

"You have a fine son, Mr Howlett."

"But Jane . . .?"

"Your wife has done very well. You can go up now."

He almost leapt at the stairs. A moment later Peter came down, his forehead furrowed in a speculative frown.

"Any idea what the trouble is?" he asked, going to the sink to scrub his hands.

Linden told him briefly what she knew.

"Mm . . . I'd better have a word with Howlett, I

think," he said thoughtfully. "He seems a decent young chap."

Within a few minutes, Tom Howlett came down again. "She'd like a cup of tea," he said tersely, opening the kitchen cupboard.

"Yes, I think we could all do with one," Peter said cheerfully. He gave Linden a meaning glance behind Tom's back. She nodded and left them alone.

Jane was leaning over the cot when Linden returned to the bedroom. She pulled back with a guilty start when she heard the door squeak, and gave Linden a defiant glare, as if daring her to make any comment.

Without the heavy maquillage of cosmetics which she normally wore and with her hair falling loosely about her face, she looked even younger than her years and curiously vulnerable. Linden busied herself with settling the baby for the night, and presently Tom Howlett brought them both a cup of tea. When he had gone, Linden saw that Jane was biting her lower lip and there was a glint of tears on her lashes.

"There you are, Mrs. Howlett. I don't think he'll disturb you tonight. You both need a good long sleep," Linden said gently. She sensed that, as soon as she had gone, Jane would burst into tears, but this was not the moment to probe the girl's secret wretchedness.

Peter was waiting for her in the hall, and after Linden had told Tom how to deal with any contingencies they left the house together.

"Did you get to the bottom of it?" she asked softly, as he opened the gate for her.

After the warmth of the house, it was cool in the silent street and she was glad of her thick grey uniform coat.

Peter produced his pipe and foraged through his pockets for matches. "I think so," he said, after a moment. "He wasn't very forthcoming at first, but I told him it was a bad start for the child if his wife is a bag of nerves. Look, come and sit in the car for a minute. It's too draughty to talk here."

Linden put her case on the motor cycle and followed him to the car. Peter switched on the interior light and lit his pipe. Then he said, "It's a fairly common case. As far as I can gather, they were really keen on each other at the beginning, more or less going steady but not in any rush to settle down. Then the baby started, and when they realised they'd have to get married at once it all went sour. They both felt trapped, I suppose?"

"Well, I can understand that," Linden put in. "But surely, if they were going to marry eventually . . ."

"Apparently Mrs. Howlett's parents made things worse by treating Tom as if he were the world's worst blackguard. Obviously they had a good deal of justification, but, instead of making the best of the situation, they kept digging at him until finally he lost his temper and burst out with something to the effect that he'd marry their daughter for the child's sake, but he wished to God he'd never set eyes on her. Unfortunately the girl overheard him and they've been barely on speaking terms ever since."

"I see," Linden said soberly. "Not very promising, is it?"

"'Fraid not. Howlett says he did his best to convince her that he hadn't meant it, but she refused to listen."

"Yet I think she still loves him," Linden said thoughtfully. "In fact I'm sure she does. The question is how to make her believe that he loves her."

"That's something I've been asking myself these last few days," Peter said quietly, reaching for her hand.

Absorbed in the Howletts' problems, Linden had completely forgotten all personal issues. Now, seeing Peter's face, she knew it was too late for any evasive tactics.

"You must have guessed last Sunday how I feel about you, Linden," he said, in a low voice. "I know this is pretty rapid, but neither of us is a susceptible teenager. Will you ... do you think you can feel the same way about me?"

Linden looked down at his hand enfolding her own. "Oh, Peter – what a very odd moment to choose," she said helplessly.

"I know – but I can't stand the suspense any longer," he said wryly. There was a long strained pause during which Linden could think of nothing to say but that it must be long past one o'clock and time they were both in bed.

"I *didn't* guess on Sunday," she managed finally. "I – I just thought you were feeling ..." She floundered uncertainly.

"Well, now that you know what I felt, think about it will you?" he said gently. Then, with sudden impatience, "Darn it! Why did I have to pick this spot to tell you? If I kiss you now, there's bound to be someone all ready to report us for unprofessional conduct. Even the owls are probably scandal-mongers in this neighbourhood."

He looked so comically furious with himself that Linden burst out laughing. "We probably ought not to be sitting in the car together. I'd better go," she said, reaching for the door handle.

"When can I see you again? Are you free at all tomorrow?"

"I don't know. You – you'd better ring me," she said awkwardly.

"Right. I'll do that. Goodnight, my dear." He was still holding her hand, and as she swung her legs out of the car, he leaned over and pressed a kiss into the palm.

It was an effort of will for Linden to get up the following morning. It had been two o'clock by the time she had got to bed, and another hour before sleep had finally claimed her. Looking at herself in the bathroom mirror, she saw that there were dark shadows under her eyes.

Arriving at the Craig house, she met Randal on the stairs.

"You look tired out," he said critically.

"I was up late." Linden's tone was frosty. She was not in the mood to accept his autocratic manner this morning.

The baby had just been fed, so Linden thought it best not to disturb her for a bath.

"I think she could sleep outside this morning. Have you got a pram yet?" she asked Paula.

"Yes, it's all ready in the hall and Randal will keep an ear open. He hasn't gone to church."

"I'll take her down then," Linden said, wrapping the infant snugly in an extra shawl.

Randal came out of the drawing room as she was tucking the baby into the expensive coach-built perambulator.

"I'll show you the way out to the garden," he said, holding open a door at the rear of the hall.

"Will you be somewhere near?" Linden asked, as they came out on to the terrace.

"Yes, over there."

Linden chose a shady spot nearby, put on the brake and adjusted the canopy.

"There's some coffee waiting for you," Randal said briskly.

"Thank you, but I really haven't time to . . ."

"Ten minutes won't wreck your schedule. Come and sit down." His fingers slid under her elbow and he marched her back to the chairs. "What time did you get to bed?" he asked, as they sat down.

"About two o'clock. Do you interrogate all your acquaintances if they look at all under the weather, Mr. Craig?"

He gave her an amused glance. "You're a touchy young thing, aren't you?"

"Not always," she said, with meaning. The coffee was too hot for her to gulp it down and escape.

"What made you take up this type of nursing?" he asked suddenly. "I thought theatre work was the popular goal."

"It is for a lot of nurses," Linden agreed. "I suppose I chose midwifery because one is more independent than in hospital. I shall probably go over to H.V. eventually – being a Health Visitor," she added explanatorily, forgetting that his seat on the committee gave him more knowledge than most laymen.

"What about marriage – where does that fit in?"

Linden looked away towards the pram. "I haven't considered that yet," she said composedly.

"Would you want to go on working if you married?"

"That would depend on my husband's view, wouldn't it?"

"Would it?" he asked dryly. "I thought marriage wasn't enough for women nowadays."

"There again, I should say it depended on their husbands. Do you disapprove of wives having outside jobs?"

"I wouldn't want to come home and cook my own supper," he said mildly.

"That wouldn't be very likely in your case, would it?" she pointed out

"Not literally, perhaps – but an efficient staff is no substitute for a full-time wife."

Linden put down her empty cup. "I must go now. Thank you for the coffee, Mr. Craig. If the baby starts to cry, perhaps you could turn it over. That's often all that's wrong."

But as she rose to leave, voices came from the drawing room, and Adela Craig stepped out on to the terrace, followed by her son and Melanie. They had evidently been to church, as Mrs. Craig was carrying a prayer book and Andrew was wearing a dark suit.

"Hello, Nurse. How's my wife getting on?" he asked pleasantly.

"Very well, Mr. Craig. I've brought Jennifer down for an airing," Linden said smiling. She was conscious that both Mrs. Craig and Melanie had noticed the two used coffee cups on the table.

As usual, Melanie was strikingly lovely in a lilac suit trimmed with a bunch of Parma violets. A provocative gleam added mystery to her tawny eyes.

"I've been invited to lunch, Randal," she said, after Andrew had gone to take a peep at his offspring. "Daddy is away for the weekend, so I'm all on my own."

"I expect Paula will be glad to see you. She's chafing at being kept upstairs," Randal remarked. "When will she be allowed out?" he asked Linden.

"I think Dr. Henderson likes his patients to stay in bed for at least eight days," Linden answered.

Mrs. Craig sat down and pulled off her grey kid gloves. "We shall definitely have to engage a nannie, Randal," she said positively. "The child was crying again last night and Andrew says he hardly slept at all. He can't be expected to sacrifice his rest indefinitely, you know."

"Particularly as his days are so arduous," Randal said coolly.

Mrs. Craig stiffened. "Nor is it fair to Paula," she went on swiftly. "I am sure Nurse will agree that proper sleep is most essential to good health. We shall all be adversely affected by a series of broken nights."

"Since Nurse Templar seems to work round the clock, I doubt if she regards us as objects of sympathy," Randal replied dryly.

Linden had no wish to be involved in a family disagreement, so she quickly excused herself and hurried away, using the side path to the drive. As she reached the corner of the drive she heard Melanie say coolly, "Coffee *à deux*, Randal? If you don't take care, she'll be setting her cap at you."

When Linden went home for tea, she found a letter lying on the mat. It was unstamped and the writing was strange to her. Puzzled, she slit open the envelope and drew out a single sheet of paper. It was dated the day before with "3 a.m." written in brackets, and it was signed *Yours – Peter.*

Sweet Linden, (he had written)

Forgive me for making a hash of things tonight and don't write me off as a clumsy oaf. I knew the first time we met that you were someone special. I realise a humdrum G.P. isn't much of a catch, but I love you, and I'm sure I could make you happy. I suppose I've rushed my fences a bit, so if you want me to, I won't say any more for a while.

Linden read the note through twice and then put it in her pocket and walked slowly to the kitchen to put on a kettle. She leaned against the table, locking and unlocking her fingers, her expression troubled.

On the only previous occasion when someone had asked her to marry him, she had known that it was impossible, and saying so had been one of the most difficult experiences of her life. But this time she didn't know what she felt. Love – the kind of love that lasted a lifetime – was supposed to be a feeling that left no room for doubt. But was it always so certain? She had known girls who, on the very eve of their weddings, had been shaken with last-minute doubts. How could one ever be sure that what one felt now, at this moment out of time, would endure for as long as one lived? And what did she feel for Peter at this moment? Liking ... respect ... attraction ... yes, all those things. But did they add up to love?

On Friday afternoon Linden was on duty at the clinic with Jill.

"You look a bit whacked, old thing," Jill said, when the relaxation class was over and they were putting the room in order.

"I've a slight headache," Linden admitted.

"Have another cup of tea. I think there's some left," Jill suggested. "Oh, by the way, I walked in on a family dust-up when I did your visit to Mrs. Craig yesterday."

Linden looked surprised. "What was wrong?"

Jill foraged in her handbag and produced a bottle of aspirins. "Here, take a couple of these," she advised. "Well, I got the impression that young Mrs. C. had been having a difference of opinion with her formidable mamma-in-law. She was almost in tears, and if looks could kill, the old girl would have felled me on the spot."

"Did you find out what the trouble was?"

"No – but I expect it was the usual difficulty. Too many cooks spoil the broth – or, in this case, the baby."

Linden swallowed the tablets and grimaced at the taste of the tea. She knew that her headache was emotional rather than physical. Peter's note was still worrying her. It was all very well for him to offer to continue their friendship as before if she needed time to clarify her reactions. Linden doubted if that were possible. Once something had been brought into the open, it was tricky to pretend that it was still unspoken.

She sighed and began to stack the cups and saucers while Jill bundled away the exercise mattresses. "Was anyone else there – at the Craig house?" she asked, over her shoulder.

"I didn't see anyone." Jill shut the cupboard door and turned the key. Then, with a thoughtful glance, she said, "Why do you ask?"

"Oh ... I just wondered if Mr. Craig was about," Linden said quickly.

"Which Mr. Craig?"

"Her husband, of course." Linden picked up the tray and carried it away to the pantry.

Jill followed with the big earthenware teapot. "Do you see much of Randal Craig when you're up there?" she asked casually.

"Not much." Linden's tone was equally careless. "I've seen Miss Fletcher several times."

But Jill was not to be deflected. "Look, Linden ... you haven't fallen for him, have you?" she asked uncertainly.

"Who ... Randal?" Linden was startled and faintly alarmed at the effort required to keep her tone light. "What a crazy idea," she said flatly.

"Is it? You've been looking pretty blue these last few days."

"Not on account of Randal." Linden managed a laugh. "Really, Jill, you seem to think the man is irresistible. Oh, lord, look at the time! I'll have to fly."

"You aren't annoyed with me, are you?" Jill asked anxiously. "It ... it's just that I'd hate to see you hurt."

Linden grinned. "Thanks – but I can look after myself."

But later, riding home, she had to admit to herself that her friend's concern for her was not as groundless as she had pretended. Somehow Randal Craig had succeeded in making her forget her original antipathy towards him until now, try as she might to ignore it, she was sharply conscious of his magnetism.

All right, the man is attractive and you feel a mild flutter – that doesn't mean you're in danger of falling in love with him, she told herself firmly.

Yet, next morning, on her way to visit Paula, she could not help wondering if Randal would be at home as he had the previous Saturday, and she knew that it was the possibility of meeting him that had prompted her to put on a clean uniform and take more than her usual care over her hair and make-up.

Paula was in the garden when Linden arrived. She was resting on the scarlet-cushioned lounger on the terrace and looking very cool and fresh in a cotton housecoat.

"I wondered if you'd come today. Is the rush over?" she asked, smiling.

"For the time being," Linden said wryly. "How are you feeling?"

"Oh ... fine." Paula smiled again, but her glance slid quickly away and there was a pucker between her brows as she looked towards the nearby pram.

Linden looked over at the baby. "I don't think she needs to be quite so muffled up now. One blanket is quite enough on a day like this," she suggested, as Paula oined her

"That's what I thought, but my mother-in-law said she might get chilled."

Linden removed the lacy quilt and the second blanket. "Oh, they're pretty tough, you know. She doesn't really need a bonnet while it's sunny." She glanced at Paula's face, then folded the blanket and said quietly, "You'll find that people smother you with advice – most of it contradictory. The best thing is just to look politely interested and then do what you feel is right. It's your baby."

They moved back to the terrace and Paula sat down with a sigh. "That's easier said than done unless one's very strong-minded," she said, with a tremor in her voice. "I wish ..." She broke off, and began nervously twisting her rings.

"Oh, everyone feels rather harassed and inadequate at first," Linden said cheerfully. "Don't worry: you'll manage beautifully once you've had time to adjust."

"I suppose so." Paula's mouth quivered and a tear trailed down her cheek.

"Good morning, Nurse."

Linden turned and found that Mrs. Craig had come

across the grass without their noticing her. She was wearing gardening gloves and carrying a trug of roses and a pair of clippers.

As Linden moved, the older woman caught sight of her daughter-in-law and said at once, "Oh, really, Paula! You must make an effort to control yourself. What is the matter *now*?"

"I shouldn't worry, Mrs. Craig. It's quite usual for people to feel depressed for a day or two at this stage," Linden said quickly and quietly. She had hoped that a good cry would relieve whatever pent-up worry or resentment was burdening the girl.

Mrs. Craig gave her a glacial look. "I have some experience of these matters you know, Nurse," she said frigidly. "Now listen to me, Paula. It's quite ridiculous for you to give way to these bouts of emotionalism. If you don't feel well, you should tell Dr. Henderson."

Paula fumbled for a handkerchief and blew her nose. "I feel perfectly well," she said, in a choked voice.

"Then please make some effort to behave normally. Poor Andrew is getting quite worried about you."

Paula sprang to her feet. "Oh, poor Andrew – that's all you ever think about!" she burst out. "Why shouldn't Andrew be worried? He's not a schoolboy any longer. He's a man – a father! You can't go on cossetting him for ever."

"Paula! you forget yourself!" For an instant, Linden thought that Mrs. Craig was going to slap her.

"I don't care. It's time someone told you the truth," the girl cried out fiercely. Then, with a tremendous effort to steady herself, she said in a shaking voice, "I love Andrew, but if I'd known what I know now I would never have married him. I don't want to live here. I want a home of my own. I don't want my baby to be brought up by a nannie. I want to look after her myself. But most of all I want a husband who isn't dominated by his mother!"

Linden had to admire the inflexible strength of will which saved Mrs. Craig from giving vent to her outrage. "You are more overwrought than I had realised, Paula," she said, with icy control. "Please go up to your room."

Linden waited for Paula to defy her, but, quite suddenly, all the girl's mettle seemed to die away and her shoulders sagged in defeat. Without a word, she turned and ran into the house.

When she had gone, there was a strained silence for some moments. Then, stripping off her gloves, Mrs. Craig said coldly, "You must excuse my daughter-in-law, Nurse. She is very highly strung, I'm afraid."

Linden hesitated before replying. It was not part of her job to intervene in family disputes, but it was clear from the vehemence of Paula's outburst that she was in a highly nervous condition, and this was bound to affect her health and upset the baby's well-being unless it was checked. As far as she could see, her best course was to tell Dr. Henderson what had happened and leave it to him to try and ease the situation.

At this point Mrs. Craig was called to the telephone and Linden made her way upstairs. She found Paula lying on the bed, her face buried in the pillow to muffle her sobs. It was some time before Linden could calm her, and even when her sobs had subsided and her breathing steadied to normal, there was still a desperate look in her eyes that made Linden half afraid to leave her.

"I'm sorry, Nurse. I – I shouldn't have made a scene. I don't know what's the matter with me," the girl said wretchedly, sipping a glass of water.

Linden patted her shoulder. "Try and have a nap," she suggested. "You're overtired, I expect."

Finally having persuaded Paula to lie down, she half closed the venetian blinds and slipped quietly out of the room.

There were voices coming from the drawing room as

she reached the foot of the stairs, and she paused, wondering if Andrew was at home and if she ought to have a tactful word with him.

"... I might have overlooked it, but to behave in such a way in front of that wretched girl. I was never so humilated in my life." The voice was Mrs. Craig's and whoever she was speaking to, she was no longer troubled to suppress her furious indignation. Too irritated by the woman's incredible egotism to realise that she was eavesdropping, Linden waited for the reply.

"I gather you don't like Nurse Templar." This time the voice was Randal's.

"I certainly do not. I wouldn't be at all surprised if she had something to do with Paula's extraordinary behaviour. Fortunately she will only be coming here for another two or three days. Oh, I daresay you don't dislike her. Men are always so blind if a girl has passable looks."

"On the contrary, I shall be very pleased when she leaves us," Randal replied.

Out in the hall, Linden flinched. She did not care what Mrs. Craig thought of her, but to hear Randal agree with the woman was curiously painful.

And then before she had time to recover herself, the drawing room door swung open and Randal came out. His eyebrows went up when he saw her, but it was clear that he had no idea what she had heard.

"Good morning," he said pleasantly.

Linden stared at him blankly a strange coldness gripping her inside. Too late she knew that what she had dismissed as a passing attraction was something far stronger and more pitiable. Blindly, refusing to see the danger, she had let herself fall in love with him.

CHAPTER FIVE

He must have seen the shiver that ran over her, as he said, "Are you all right?"

She stiffened. "Perfectly, thank you." Her voice came out harsh and too loud. Before he could say any more, she almost ran to the door.

The rest of the day passed in a kind of blur until at last she was free to go home and rest and think. It was useless to persuade herself that nothing had happened ... that love didn't come like a thunderclap ... that she must force herself to be sensible. That moment of self-revelation in the Craigs' hall had been too clear to allow any further deception.

I can't love him! I won't! she thought desperately. But she knew that she did love him, and it frightened her.

She was preparing her supper when the bell rang. It was Peter.

"You don't look too pleased to see me." He was smiling, but there was a flicker of anxiety in his eyes.

"Oh, it's you. I – I thought it was another call," Linden said, hastily masking her dismay. "Come in."

He followed her into the sitting room. "Are you free this evening?"

Her immediate reaction was to say no. Then she wondered if an evening with the Carburys could be worse than being alone.

"I'm on call if I'm needed," she said cautiously.

"Well, come and have supper with us. You can let them know where to find you."

Linden hesitated. An hour ago, she had been longing

for solitude, but already the flat seemed like a prison. "All right," she said doubtfully. "I'll follow you up when I've phoned."

Linden made a gallant effort to hide her inner conflict that evening, but Peter must have sensed that she was on edge, or else he was waiting for some definite sign of encouragement. Either way, he avoided any word or gesture that could be taken to refer to their last meeting, and although his mother several times left them alone together, he did not even look at her with anything beyond casual friendliness.

Watching him as he lounged in a deep easy chair, Linden wondered what made people fall in love with each other so haphazardly. It seemed incredible now that she could ever have debated with herself whether she loved Peter. Yet why, if he loved her, did she fail to respond?

"You're looking very solemn," he said, smiling at her.

She jumped. "Oh ... I was day-dreaming. Sorry."

He leaned forward to knock out his pipe on the hearth. "Blessed is the woman who doesn't chatter incessantly. By the way, when is your next long weekend?"

"The one after next," she said.

"Going home?"

"I'm not sure yet, but I expect so." She stood up. "I'd better get back now. It's after ten."

They went into the kitchen where Mrs. Carbury was taking a batch of soda bread from the oven. Linden thanked her for her hospitality and then Peter accompanied her to the gate.

"You're not overdoing things, are you? You look a shade drawn," he said gravely, pushing the motor cycle on to the road for her.

"I'm fine," she said shortly. Then: "I'm sorry, I didn't mean to snap. I'm just a bit tired, that's all."

He touched her hand, and something in his face made her nerves tighten. But he only smiled and said goodnight.

Linden woke up next morning with a heavy sense of apprehension. Her first call was to the young Howletts.

A marked change had come over Jane Howlett since the birth of her child. Her mouth had lost its petulant droop and in some strange way the baby seemed to have restored her self-respect. What had formerly been an unwanted anonymous burden was now a source of almost inordinate pride, and she no longer troubled to conceal her gratification. Her husband, too, seemed delighted by his infant's size and vigour. Being on shift work, he was at home when Linden called, and watched the child being bathed with an interest that was curiously touching. It seemed that little Paul James Howlett was not, after all, an unwelcome and resented baby.

When Linden reached the Craig house, her nerves were as taut as a high wire. She felt sure that Randal would be at home and that she was certain to see him – and she both dreaded and wanted the meeting.

Half an hour later, she left the house without even hearing his voice.

On Tuesday she made her final call, and, as they said goodbye, Paula slipped a small package into her hand.

"I hope you'll like it. You've been so nice to me and I do appreciate it," she said shyly.

Linden did not open the present until she went back to the flat at lunchtime. As far as she knew, Paula had not yet been into the town, and she wondered who had chosen and bought the gift.

Slitting open the wax-paper, she found a shallow leather case with a spring clip fastening. Inside, on a black silk lining stamped in gold with the name of the town's leading silversmiths, was a most charming evening bracelet of pinchbeck and coral. By a strange chance, it was very like a pair of Victorian earrings which an elderly aunt had left to her in her teens, and had she received it in any other way, Linden would have been delighted. But although it was by far the most lavish and tasteful token of appreciation that she had ever received for her services, Linden felt an odd distaste for it. Wearing it would only remind her of an episode which she knew it would be wiser to forget – which she *must* forget.

She put the box away in the bottom of a drawer and wondered how long it would be before she could look at it again without this wretched inner ache.

Several weeks passed and Linden did her best never to think of the Craigs. She told herself that falling out of love was like following a strict diet. To let herself think about Randal would be like trying to quell one's hunger while surrounded by forbidden delicacies. It was all a question of mental discipline, and, after a while, the longing would gradually ebb.

During this time, she saw Peter quite often, but he made no attempt to speak of his feelings for her. This worried Linden a little and she wondered if she ought to tell him that she could never be more than a friend to him. But it was difficult to broach the subject when he was so steadfastly skirting it.

To help out another nurse who particularly wanted to be off duty then, Linden had switched her long weekend. Two days before she was finally due to go home, her morning post included a large white envelope addressed in an unfamiliar hand. Inside was a printed invitation to attend Jennifer Craig's christening that Sunday. On the bottom of the card Paula had written: *I do hope you will be able to come. We should so much like to have you with us.*

Linden's instinct was to write a polite refusal, explaining that she had arranged to stay with her parents. But, even as she put the card aside and finished her breakfast, the temptation to accept began to undermine her resolution.

Perhaps she would have been able to resist it, but later in the day she met Paula wheeling the perambulator, and was forced out of normal courtesy to stop the motor cycle and speak to her.

"You are coming on Sunday, I hope?" Paula said, almost immediately.

And because, suddenly, her longing to see Randal again was stronger than her will, Linden rashly committed herself.

Friday and Saturday were miserable days. Her parents had been very disappointed when she telephoned to tell them of her change of plan, and she was furious with herself for weakening so easily.

Instead of being held immediately after the morning service, the christening had been arranged for mid-afternoon, and Linden guessed that it would be quite a big social event. All through the morning her nervousness grew stronger, and she bitterly regretted accepting the invitation. Even if Paula sincerely wanted her to be there, she had no doubt that the other members of the family would treat her with pointed coolness.

Because she never wore a hat other than her jaunty uniform beret, she had had to buy one specially for the occasion, and as she took it out of the tissue paper some of her confidence returned. At least no one would be able to criticise her clothes.

Guessing that there was sure to be a superabundance of flowery caps and wide picture-brims, she had chosen a pimento-red straw with a broad brim that shaded her face. It had been unjustifiably expensive, but she knew that it was the kind of hat which her sister Louise would have approved, its vivid colour a wonderful accent for the simple cream linen suit which was one of Louise's cast-offs.

She reached the church about ten minutes before the christening was due to begin. The road was lined with big glossy cars, and people were clustered about the lychgate exchanging greetings before they moved up the path.

Linden was conscious of several curious glances as she walked to the church door, and she felt uncomfortably solitary. Then, as the people ahead of her moved slowly inside the church to take their places, she saw Randal standing at the end of the central aisle and caught in her breath. Carefully avoiding looking at him, she followed an expensively scented woman in pearl grey wild silk, hoping to hide behind her.

"So you came."

Linden's pulses jerked as the familiar voice spoke in her ear and a firm hand slid under her elbow. She looked up at him, her cheeks growing hot, her heart thumping wildly.

"I've kept a place for you further down." His fingers tightening on her arm, Randal guided her forward. It seemed to Linden that the aisle was a mile long and that, on both sides, heads were turning to appraise her. At the second pew from the front, Randal indicated two empty places and she murmured something unintelligible and stepped quickly inside.

It seemed to Linden that the service had scarcely begun before it was over. She had assumed that Randal would be the child's godfather, but this duty was taken by a young man whom she had never seen before, and Randal was at her side throughout the ceremony. Once, while everyone's attention was on the font, she ventured a swift glance at him, but looked quickly away again.

Outside the church, a photographer was waiting to take pictures. People strolled back to their cars, the women commenting on how good the baby had been, not even whimpering when the water was sprinkled on its head.

"The car's round the corner. We'll cut across here,"

Randal said, leading her along a side path between the old grey tombstones.

"Oh ... but shouldn't you ... aren't you ...?" she began.

He arched an amused eyebrow. "They all know the way. I've been detailed to look after you."

She stiffened. "You will look after Nurse Templar, won't you, Randal?" She almost heard Paula saying it.

In the car, Randal said, "It was nice of you to come. I imagine you get asked to dozens of these affairs."

"Sometimes," Linden said briefly.

He waited at the junction for a couple of cars to pass. "How many infants have you helped to produce since we last saw you?"

"Oh ... about a dozen, I suppose." She fiddled with the clasp of her bag for a moment. "How is your sister-in-law getting on now?"

He glanced at her. "I think she'd be happier in a home of her own," he said dryly.

"Isn't that possible?"

"Everything is possible," he said, with a shrug.

Linden's mouth twisted. Not everything, she thought bleakly.

He had driven slowly and when they reached the house the cars of the christening party and several guests were already parked in the drive. Linden had supposed that she would never see the house again, and when they passed the spot where she had fallen from her motor cycle she remembered with an inner pang how Randal had picked her up and held her close to him.

The drawing room was full of white flowers, beautifully arranged. A long table, with the frosty white christening cake in the centre, was set with plates of appetising sandwiches and cakes.

"Nurse Templar! I'm so glad you could come." Paula came forward smiling, and took Linden's hand.

She was looking very pretty in a printed silk dress and shady hat, and there was a genuine warmth in her greeting. Andrew Craig made himself equally agreeable.

More people were arriving and Paula had to move away to welcome them. Randal had been buttonholed by an elderly man with a moustache. For a few moments Linden was left by herself. She saw Mrs. Craig glance at her from across the room and then deliberately turn away.

"Hello again. I didn't know you knew the Craigs." A pleasant-faced boy of about twenty had separated himself from the incoming stream and was beaming down on her.

"Oh ... hello." Linden had never seen him before in her life, but at least he would save her from standing on her own. She wondered how long it would take him to realise his mistake.

"Nothing stronger than tea?" the boy said in an undertone, looking towards the table. "I thought one usually wetted the baby's head or something. I say, are you going to the Baxters' tennis party on Wednesday?"

"Er ... no, I don't think so," Linden said awkwardly.

"Oh, too bad. You play, don't you?"

"Yes, but not very well." Over his shoulder she saw Melanie Fletcher arriving.

Randal came back with two cups of tea and some sandwiches, all expertly balanced.

"Hello, John," he said coolly. "I think your mother wants a word with you. She's over there."

"Oh – does she?" The youth glanced across the room. "Well ... see you later, I hope," he said to Linden.

"Do you know him?" Randal asked, when he had left them.

Linden accepted a cup of tea. "No. I think he mistook me for someone else."

Randal's eyebrows went up. "Or was he trying out a line?" he said, looking amused.

"Oh, hardly. I must be at least five years older than he is."

He laughed aloud. "Is that such an obstacle? Lads of that age usually are attracted by someone more sophisticated."

"Are they? But I'm not particularly sophisticated," she answered.

"No, you aren't, are you?" There was a gleam of mockery in his eyes. "But you probably look it to him. Let's move out on to the terrace. It's getting crowded in here."

Outside, Linden said lightly, "Did you pursue older women when you were his age?"

"At nineteen? It's a long time ago. I imagine I went through all the usual phases."

"I can't . . ." she stopped short.

"Well?"

Linden hesitated, then plunged. "I can't imagine you being at all – callow," she said, not looking at him.

"Can't you?" He was laughing at her again.

Without looking, she knew the expression on his face – the narrowed eyes, the sardonic tilt of his mouth. "But then you are inclined to regard me as slightly sub-human in all respects, aren't you?" he added.

Linden's eyes widened and she stared at him. "No . . . of course I don't," she said startled.

"Oh, there you are, Randal!" Melanie came out of the drawing room, the light breeze catching the folds of her skirt. Surprisingly, she gave Linden a charming smile. "I almost didn't recognise you out of uniform, Nurse. What a pretty hat. Did you find it in Melchester?"

Linden was so staggered by this sudden cordiality

that, for a moment, she gaped. "Yes ... yes, I did," she said recovering herself.

"I adore that shade of red – but of course I can never wear it because of my hair," Melanie said, with a gesture. "Randal, can I have a cigarette? I've run out."

Randal offered his cigarette case to them both. He held the lighter for Linden, then for the other girl. Melanie's fingers rested on his wrist as she bent to the flame.

"Are you free today, or are you likely to be called out suddenly?" she asked Linden.

"I'm free till midnight tomorrow." Linden tried to sound friendly, but she knew she was being stiff.

"I wish I had a vocation," Melanie said lightly. "It's so old-fashioned not to be at all ambitious, but I think it saves complications when one marries. I don't think men really like sharing their wives with a career. You wouldn't, would you, Randal? It's one of your pet themes."

"I'm not in favour of it," he said, without emphasis. "Excuse me a moment, will you?"

He went into the house and Melanie opened her bag and retouched her lips.

"Shall we stroll?" she said pleasantly, with a gesture towards the garden.

They walked across the grass, and Linden wondered if she was being unnecessarily suspicious to feel wary of this sudden alteration in the other girl's attitude.

"I love your suit," Melanie said, glancing at it. "You know – it sounds quite absurd – but I was a little intimidated when you came here professionally. People who are terribly efficient make me feel so inadequate."

Linden said nothing. It was possible, of course, that Melanie's outward assurance was a screen for inner uncertainty. But it didn't seem likely. Melanie went on chatting until they came to the edge of the little lake.

"Randal's very attractive, isn't he?" she said suddenly.

Linden watched a dragonfly skimming the surface of the water. So this was what it was about?

"I suppose he is," she said detachedly.

Melanie dropped the end of her cigarette into the reeds. "Of course that charm can be misleading if one doesn't know him well," she said casually. "I don't think he realises the effect he has on people."

Linden made no comment, wondering why Melanie thought it necessary to warn her off. Perhaps she was not as sure of Randal as she could wish. Perhaps she wasn't sure at all and was taking no chances.

About five o'clock people began to leave and Linden had a few words with Paula and her husband before saying goodbye. She was looking about for her hostess when Randal came up and said, "Leaving? I'll run you home."

"Oh, please – you really needn't bother."

"Don't be silly. You can't walk all that way," he said, rather abruptly.

"I haven't said goodbye to Mrs. Craig."

"She's somewhere in the garden. I'll tell her you were looking for her."

He was silent on the drive to the flat and Linden could find nothing to say. She knew that, as soon as she was alone, she would feel more wretched than before, and she wished that she had had the sense to go home for the weekend. As they entered the estate her throat was tight and she felt stupidly close to tears.

Randal stopped the car outside the flats, but left the engine running.

"What are you doing with yourself this evening?"

Linden's heart lurched, but she made herself answer casually. "Oh . . . I'll probably walk along the river."

He put the car in gear again and accelerated.

"Where are we going?" she asked sharply.

"You can walk by the sea with me instead," he said calmly.

It was the kind of reprieve for which she had not dared to hope, but she said crisply, "Do you often shanghai people like this?"

"When it's necessary."

"Won't they wonder where you are?"

"Possibly." He slowed the car again and glanced at her. "I'll take you back if you really don't want to come."

Linden's cheeks flamed. She might have known that he would turn the tables on her. "No, I think it would be very pleasant," she said evenly.

They reached the coast a little after six o'clock and Randal parked the car on the grassy headland. "We'll have dinner in Stanmouth. There's a very good restaurant there," he said, helping her out.

She left her hat and bag in the car. Fortunately her heels were not too high to make walking uncomfortable, and there was a track near the cliff's edge.

"It must have been fun living so near the sea when you were a child," she said presently.

"I didn't see much of it, except during the school holidays."

"Oh, yes, I suppose you wouldn't. I'd forgotten that. You were at boarding school, weren't you?"

"How did you know that?" he asked curiously.

"I think the Carburys mentioned it."

"Peter Carbury?"

"Yes – or his mother. She's been very kind to me since I came here."

"Has Peter been kind too?"

Linden ignored his tone. "Everyone has," she said levelly.

"I remember the Carburys' house. I had tea there once or twice as a schoolboy. They were wonderful teas. Great hunks of fruit cake and lots of cream. None of those genteel scones that one could swallow in a mouthful."

Linden smiled. "My grandmother used to take us to a café. I always chose baked beans and Devonshire splits."

"Is that what you'd like tonight?"

She laughed and shook her head. "Beans never taste the same now."

"What were you like as a little girl?" he asked. "Fat and pigtailed, or one of the scrawny species?"

"Just untidy and clumsy, I think. I could never move anywhere without knocking something over. I must have driven my parents mad. When I first thought of taking up nursing they had a fit. I suppose they had visions of my giving people overdoses of drugs or dropping the babies."

"One would never think it to look at you now."

"One can't ever tell very much from the way people look. I wouldn't have suspected that you were rather lawless as a boy." He looked puzzled, so she said, "Mrs. Carbury said you were very polite but the leader of several escapades, and now you're a councillor – very sedate."

"I more or less inherited that from my father," he said carelessly. "There's always been a Craig in local government since my great-grandfather's time, so the people in my world are pretty well conditioned to voting for us."

"Did you want to take on the family business?"

"Fortunately, yes. Andrew has never had much leaning in that direction." He glanced at his watch. "Shall we head for our dinner?"

The streets of Stanmouth were thronged with holidaymakers returning from the beach for their evening meal, and Linden wondered if, at the height of the season, Randal would be able to get a table at the restaurant he had mentioned. She still found it hard to believe that she was really spending the evening with him, and every minute was precious. Why had he brought her? She refused to speculate: content to live for the moment and leave all such ponderings until later.

The restaurant was part of an hotel, but was open to non-residents. It was like an enormous conservatory with trellises of climing plants screening the tables, most of which were already taken.

"I booked a table for two. My name is Craig," Randal said to the manageress who was standing near the entrance.

"Oh, yes, Mr. Craig. This way, please." She led them to a small table which overlooked the promenade.

Randal settled Linden in her chair and a waitress handed them menus.

"What would you like?" he asked.

"Can I leave it to you?" Linden suggested.

While he was choosing their meal, she watched the people passing along the esplanade. Across the roadway, the neon lights outlining the dome of the pier pavilion came on and an attendant unlocked the turnstile. So he had reserved the table earlier, Linden thought. Had he taken for granted that she would come with him? Or had the evening been planned for someone else? In spite of her resolve not to probe his motives, the possibility that she was a substitute put an edge of bitterness on her enjoyment.

They talked throughout the meal, but only of general subjects, and, when the coffee came, Randal sat silent, watching the passers-by. Do I bore him? Linden wondered miserably.

When they left the restaurant, she expected him to go back to the car. But he suggested a walk on the pier. As they passed the pavilion they could hear the music of the show going on inside.

"Are you warm enough?" Randal asked.

"Yes, perfectly, thank you." Linden averted her eyes from an embrace going on in one of the shelters. What is the matter with me tonight? I'm as stilted as a shy twelve-year-old, she thought vexedly.

At the end of the pier some anglers were watching their lines and a small boy was glued to a penny-in-the-slot telescope.

"It'll be warmer round the corner," Randal said. Suddenly, and without even looking at her, he caught her left hand and held it.

To Linden, his touch was like an electric contact, and her whole body stiffened. Dazzled by the late evening sunlight which bathed the west side of the pier she experienced an instant of the most intense happiness. But it lasted only a second. Almost immediately the swift surge of delight died away, to be replaced with awkwardness and doubt.

"Like to sit down for a while?" Randal asked, indicating an empty shelter. They did so, and he freed her hand to produce cigarettes.

"I wouldn't mind living here," he remarked, when they had lit up. "Not in Stanmouth itself, but up on the cliffs where we were this afternoon."

"Don't you like your present house?" Linden asked, surprised to find that her voice was steady. Her fingers had trembled as she took the cigarette and she was sure he must have noticed.

"Not particularly. I was on the point of moving when Andrew got married." He saw the puzzled look on her face, and said, "You must think it rather an odd set-up, don't you?"

Linden hesitated. "I did wonder why your brother and his wife didn't have a home of their own," she admitted diffidently.

"They could if Andrew decided to pull his weight at the works or settle to some other worthwhile job," Randal said, with a shrug. "Unfortunately my stepmother has encouraged him to think he's entitled to a life of leisure. I'd hoped that marriage might do the trick, but it hasn't worked out that way. Paula's a nice little creature, but she isn't a match for Adela." He turned his head and gave her an amused glance. "He would have done better with someone like you behind him."

Linden wasn't sure what to make of this remark. "If you must know, Mrs. Craig terrifies me," she said frankly.

He laughed. "Possibly, but I don't think you'd let her dominate you."

Linden watched a gull swooping over the sea. "I thought you did most of the dominating," she said quietly. "Everyone seems to defer to you."

"You sound as if that annoys you."

"It's not my business, is it?" she answered without expression.

He was silent for a while and she knew he was watching her. Then he took her hand again and said softly, "I think this conversation is taking the wrong tack. Let's change the subject."

Linden flickered a wary glance at him. "Oughtn't we to be going soon?" she said quickly.

"Why? Are you under orders to be in bed by ten?"

"No, of course not, but—"

His thumb moved gently over the back of her hand. So slight a caress, but it made her heart plunge wildly.

"Oh, look – a motorboat!" She jumped up, almost wrenching her hand away, and walked quickly to the rail to watch the speeding craft.

"Is it the first time you've seen one?" Randal's voice was wickedly derisive as he came to stand beside her.

"No, of course not. I just—"

"You had an uneasy feeling that I might be going to kiss you."

Linden swung round to face him. "It never occurred to me!" she flared hotly.

His mouth lifted at the corner and his eyes were brilliant with mockery. "It certainly occurred to me," he said smoothly.

Her cheeks flamed. "Really, Mr. Craig—"

"Why not?" he cut in swiftly. "Do you find the idea so distasteful?"

Linden gave him what she hoped was a withering glance and turned to walk away. But her heel, catching in the worn slats of the pier, almost sent her flying. She recovered her balance before Randal could reach her, but there had been an ominous splintering sound and, looking down, she saw that the heel had cracked.

"Let me see." As she slipped her foot out of the shoe, Randal bent and picked it up. "I'm sorry," he said quietly. "I suppose that was mainly my fault."

"It isn't important," she said resignedly. "I forgot the slats."

"Can you hobble as far as the turnstile? I'll go ahead and bring the car over."

"Thank you." She took the shoe from him and tested the broken heel. It would just about bear her weight for the length of the pier.

She watched him stride away, furious at her own ineptitude. It wasn't the first time someone had tried to flirt with her, so why had she let it fluster her? How easily Louise would have dealt with him. *She* wouldn't have made an idiot of herself.

Randal was waiting at the turnstile when she reached it. He took her arm and helped her to the car, but his touch was quite impersonal now.

"If you'll let me have the shoe, I'll get it repaired for you," he said, as they left.

"It really doesn't matter. I don't like them very much anyway, and I've got several other pairs."

He switched on the sidelights. "You're very forbearing. Most women would be furious."

"It would probably have broken soon anyway. I may have escaped a sprained ankle."

"You escaped something." There was laughter in his voice again. "By the way, we're having a party next month for Paula's birthday. Did she mention it to you? No? I expect she forgot. The invitations are late because we weren't sure whether she would feel up to it. I hope you'll come."

"I doubt if I shall be free," Linden said cautiously.

"It's a fortnight on Friday. Can't you get one of the others to stand in for you?"

"It depends how busy we are, but thank you for asking me," she said politely.

But why had he asked her? Because, in spite of their clash on the pier, he genuinely wanted to see her again? Or because she was a pawn in some complex game he was playing?

He saw her to the door and insisted on taking her shoe, in spite of her protests.

"It's the least I can do," he said firmly.

Linden listened to his footsteps going downstairs, then slowly closed the door. The more she knew of him, the less she understood him.

On Wednesday evening, Linden was washing her smalls when Peter called.

"I was passing and saw your light on, so I thought I'd look in," he said smiling.

She hesitated, wondering if anyone had seen him come to her door. "Oh . . . come in," she said doubtfully.

He must have read her thoughts as, when she had closed the door, he said, "Oh, to blazes with discretion for once. Do you realise how long it is since I've seen you?"

"It wasn't only that. I'm expecting a call tonight."

Peter fiddled with his car keys, his expression troubled. "Look, Linden, I can't keep this up," he said abruptly. "I can't be content with hardly seeing you except when we're working together." He thrust the keys into his pocket and reached for her hands. "I must have some idea how you feel about me, darling," he said huskily.

"Oh, Peter – please don't!" She tried to free herself, but his hold was too firm and she was forced to meet his eyes, her own full of sadness and regret.

He thought she was still concerned about his coming to the flat. "Don't you see? If we were engaged, I could come here without comment," he said quickly.

Linden bit her lip. She had made up her mind to tell Peter the truth – or part of it – as soon as she saw him again. But she hadn't expected him to burst in on her tonight, and she hadn't expected to have to break it to him so bluntly.

"Peter ... I like you so much," she said unhappily. "But I can't get engaged to you – ever."

He looked bewildered. "But I thought—"

"I should have told you sooner. It was very wrong of me, but you see—" She broke off, hating herself for hurting him and yet knowing it must be a clean break.

He let her go and turned to the window. "You mean there's someone else?" he said flatly.

"In a way."

He swung round again. "In a way? I don't understand you."

"I ... yes, there is someone else."

There was a pause while he stared at her searchingly. "Look, if you don't care for me ... well, that's enough. You don't have to make up something to spare my pride," he said at last.

"I'm not. It's true," she said haltingly.

"It wasn't true that day we went to Northbeach," he said with conviction.

"I didn't know it then."

"You mean it's some chap you knew in London."

"I – oh, please, don't let's have an inquest. You must know I hate telling you this."

"There isn't much to have an inquest on," he said wryly. "You can't help the way you feel. I suppose I asked for it. Have you got a cigarette?"

"Yes, of course." She fumbled in her bag for her case and offered it to him. He struck a match and she saw that his hand was unsteady.

"So you'll be leaving us, I suppose," he said, in an empty tone.

"Leaving? No ... that is ..." A wave of crimson suffused her face and throat and she turned to find an ashtray, but not quite quickly enough.

"Linden, you're hiding something," he said sharply. "Are you in some kind of trouble?"

"Of course not – what trouble could I be in?" She tried to sound astonished, but it wasn't very successful.

He put his hand on her arm and said gently, "Can't you tell me the truth?"

"I have, Peter. You're imagining things."

"I don't think I am," he said quietly.

The bell rang and Linden drew in her breath. "It must be Mrs. Grant from next door," she whispered. "If she sees you here, she'll tell the whole neighbourhood. You'd better go in the kitchen till I've got rid of her."

Peter opened his mouth to object, but Linden shook her head and frowned. "You don't know what a gossip she is." She pushed him towards the kitchen.

The bell rang a second time, and, hurriedly smoothing her hair and trying to look composed, Linden opened the door.

"Good evening. I've brought your shoe back," Randal said, walking in.

"Oh ... thank you," Linden stammered.

"Have you just come off duty?"

137

"No, I'm expecting a call." She flashed an anxious glance towards the kitchen. "It – it was very kind of you to get it mended so quickly."

"What's the matter?" He had intercepted her look. "Something cooking?"

Before Linden could answer, the kitchen door opened and Peter came out. "Oh, hello, Craig," he said calmly. Then to Linden: "The pan on the stove looks as if it's about to boil over."

"Oh, heavens – the handkerchiefs," she exclaimed, hurrying to rescue them.

The water was already frothing over the rim and she spent a few moments draining the steaming handkerchiefs and mopping the stove. When she returned to the sitting room, the two men were discussing the current test match. If Randal had seen anything odd in Peter's presence in the flat, he did not show it.

"Well, I won't hang about if you're on call," he said pleasantly. "Oh, this is a note from Paula about the dance." He handed her an envelope and moved towards the door.

Linden let him out and glanced at Peter. It was clear that he had no intention of leaving yet.

"So it's Craig," he said flatly, after some moments.

"Craig?" she repeated uneasily.

There was a kind of wry humour in his eyes as he looked at her. "I thought you had more sense, Linden."

She put Paula's note on the table unopened and tidied some books and magazines. "I don't know what you're getting at."

"Yes, you do, my sweet. You think you've fallen for Craig." He sighed. "I suppose I might have known it when you said you were on their case."

"Aren't you jumping to some rather extraordinary conclusions?" Linden said distantly. "I – I damaged one of my shoes when I went to the baby's christening. They had it mended for me and he brought it back.

That hardly seems grounds for ... for thinking I'm interested in him."

"All right – deny it!" he challenged. "Say you don't give a damn for the fellow and I'll believe you."

"Oh, Peter, you're making this worse for us both," she exclaimed.

"You see? You can't," he retorted. "Look, I don't blame you for taking a toss for him. God knows, you aren't the first. There's something about the man that seems to bowl women over like ninepins. But you must know there isn't any future in it."

"Thank you," she said coldly.

"I didn't mean it like that."

"I don't care how you meant it, Peter. I just don't want to discuss it."

"You mean you don't want to admit that it's just a crazy infatuation. You hardly know him – or do you? Have you been out with him?"

The telephone rang. Linden snatched up the receiver. "Nurse Templar speaking." She had never been more glad to receive a call. "All right, Mr. Linton, I'll be round right away." She turned to Peter. "I'm sorry, but I must go at once."

Peter waited while she collected her things and scribbled a note to put on the door in case anyone else needed her during the evening.

"I'm sorry," he said quietly, as she fastened it in place. "I shouldn't have started all this when you've got a job on."

"Oh, it doesn't matter. I – I wish it could be different."

"It may be," he said. "I'm not giving up, Linden. Not to Randal Craig."

Linden pulled on her gloves. There was no time now to try and make him understand.

"Goodnight, Peter." She slipped quickly past him and ran down the stairs.

Two days later, Linden met Mrs. Carbury in the town. She was looking for a slip among the rails of filmy petticoats in Marks & Spencer when the older woman touched her shoulder and said, "Hello, my dear. How are you?"

"Oh ... hello. I'm fine, thanks." Linden wondered if Peter had told his mother how matters stood.

"Isn't that pretty?" Mrs. Carbury said, looking at the rose-printed nylon waist slip which Linden had been examining. "I wish I had a daughter. They make such charming clothes for young girls nowadays. Are you going to buy it?"

"Yes, I think so. I need one to go under a party dress," Linden said, looking for the salesgirl.

"Oh, a special occasion?"

"The Craigs have asked me to a dance – if I can get the night off."

"I should think it will be great fun. They do a lot of entertaining, I believe." Mrs. Carbury waited while Linden made her purchase. "I've been rather extravagant this afternoon. I've bought myself two new dresses," she said, brandishing her carriers. "Are you in a hurry or can we have a cup of tea together?"

Linden hesitated, ostensibly to look at her watch. Even if Peter hadn't told her anything, Mrs. Carbury must have seen that he was upset. Would she try to intercede for him?

"Yes, I can manage half an hour," she said.

They crossed the road and went to a popular café. Mrs. Carbury propped her parcels under the table, ordered tea and toast and peeled off her short grey gloves. She was looking very attractive in grey and white tie silk with a white hat on her crisp grey hair. Linden wondered inconsequently if she would ever marry again.

They chattered about clothes for some minutes. Then Constance Carbury said suddenly, "Look, my dear, we may as well clear the air. I know that Peter asked you to marry him and that you turned him down. I hope you aren't feeling that you have to avoid me in future."

Linden coloured slightly. "I was feeling a bit uncomfortable," she admitted. "You've been so kind to me. It isn't much of a return – to make Peter unhappy."

"Well, I confess that I'd hoped you were the girl for him." She contemplated the cake trolley and chose a butterscotch twist. "He seems to think your decision may not be final," she said, after a moment.

"I'm afraid it is," Linden said miserably. "Did – did he tell you the reason?"

Mrs. Carbury nodded. "I'm sure he didn't intend to betray your confidence, but he was distressed and angry and blurted it out."

"I suppose you think I'm a complete fool?"

"No, I don't. Much the same thing happened to me once."

"But I thought . . ."

"Oh, I was in love with my husband. He wasn't a second best. The other thing happened several years before I met him, and by that time I'd got over it. The man married someone else. People say you don't 'get over' love – not if it *is* love, as distinct from infatuation. I think you can. If I'd married Phillip I would probably have been just as happy as I was with John, or happier, or quite wretched. One can never tell until afterwards. I think the important thing is to take the chances in life, to gamble a little. It's the chances one has missed that one always regrets, you know."

"I suppose so," Linden said thoughtfully.

After they had parted, she thought over what Mrs. Carbury had said. It occurred to her that in all her encounters with Randal she had been too much on edge, too busy worrying about motives and hidden meanings and possible pitfalls to enjoy the present. From the very first she had been at pains to deny his attraction and, later, she had taken for granted that she was going to be hurt.

Now, in a sudden excess of recklessness, she decided it was time she stopped retreating from the situation. If Randal was only amusing himself – well, she would meet him on his terms.

This improvident mood lasted the rest of the week, and instead of wondering if she was being foolish to go to the party, Linden worried that something might happen to keep her away. She had spoken to Mrs. Langley about having the evening off, and providing no emergencies occurred, the matter was arranged.

Linden had half expected Peter to call on her again, but she saw nothing of him or of Randal. On the night of the party, she was almost ready to leave when Jill looked in.

"Heavens! You *are* dressed to kill," her friend exclaimed admiringly.

"Do I look all right?"

"Marvellous! Positively stunning."

"Yes, I think this dress is rather successful," Linden said with satisfaction. Having decided to cut a dash, she had telephoned Louise and asked her to scour the shops for a really breathtaking dress. Her sister, intrigued by Linden's urgency, had promised to do her best, and the result of her search had arrived by parcel post the day before.

Knowing Louise's impeccable taste, Linden had been confident that her choice would not be disappointing. But the dress was even lovelier than she had expected. It was made of shimmering white organza exquisitely printed with enormous magnolia blossoms. Louise had not enclosed the bill and Linden felt sure that it must have been a ruinous price, but for once she did not care. Whatever magnificent creation Melanie Fletcher might be wearing, it couldn't possibly overshadow this drifting green and white gown with its demurely tucked bodice and cloud of floor-length folds.

"Sounds like your taxi," Jill said, going to the window. "Yes, it is. Well, good luck, old thing. Even the Craigs should be staggered by that little number. Lucky you! I wish I were going on the razzle."

Linden laughed. Her cheeks were flushed with colour and her eyes very bright. Jill thought they had an almost feverish glitter and supposed it was her friend's excitement that made her laughter sound a shade brittle.

CHAPTER SIX

In the cool darkness of the taxi, Linden shivered and drew her white silk shawl closer about her shoulders. Finding herself sitting bolt upright, she made a conscious effort to relax and breathe slowly and deeply. But relaxation in moments of stress was easier to preach than to practice, she discovered. As the taxi turned into Pine Avenue, her heart was beating very fast, and she felt slightly sick.

The house was ablaze with light and there were Chinese lanterns flickering around the lake like crimson and sapphire moons. As she stepped out of the taxi, she could hear music coming from the open windows of the drawing room. She paid the driver, lifted her swirling skirts and climbed the steps to the door.

Mrs. Craig and her daughter-in-law were standing in the hall, and Linden nearly laughed aloud at the startled expression on the older woman's face as she recognised her guest. For once she was almost gracious.

"I'll show you where to put your wrap," Paula said, leading the way upstairs. "What a ravishing dress. You didn't get *that* in Melchester."

"No, London. You look very pretty yourself – for a careworn mum," Linden said teasingly.

Paula made a face. "My waist is still two inches more than it ought to be."

"Oh, you'll soon lose that," Linden assured her. "How's Jennifer?"

"Sleeping – I hope! Mason's niece is keeping an eye on her. Do you mind if I leave you to prink? Adela likes to be awfully formal and receive the guests on the doorstep."

"Of course not."

There were already several fur wraps on the wide bed, and Linden folded her shawl and turned to the dressing-table to check her make-up. I ought to have gone the whole hog and bought some false eyelashes, she thought with a stifled laugh. Tonight her hair was loose, and, with misty-green shadow on her eyelids and the long coral earrings swinging gently against her throat, she felt almost a stranger to herself.

Several women were coming up the stairs when she went on to the landing. They were friends of Adela Craig, all wrapped in mink with expensively blue-rinsed coiffures. She waited for them to pass her and smiled. Then she went down the stairs, amusedly aware that they were impressed by her dress and wondering who she was.

Then, at the bend of the staircase, she saw Randal. He was standing in the drawing room doorway, tall and lean and very masculine in his immaculate dinner jacket. For a moment, as he turned his head and looked up at her, Linden's confidence ebbed and she gripped the rail of the banisters, wanting to turn back, afraid of the role she had cast for herself. It was only a momentary weakening, because at the same moment there was the glisten of emerald moiré at the door and Linden saw Melanie arriving.

The sight of the other girl was the added challenge she needed. Deliberately, like an actress making her entrance, she swept down the last of the stairs and held out both hands to Randal.

"Good evening," she said sweetly. She had hoped to catch him off his guard, but although his eyebrows lifted a fraction, he betrayed no surprise. His fingers closed firmly over hers and he gave a slight bow.

"You're very dazzling tonight," he said smoothly.

"Thank you." She withdrew her hands and gave him a brilliant smile, before glancing into the drawing room.

Now that she had sailed over the first hurdle, she was surprised to find it much easier than she had expected.

"Let me get you a drink," he suggested, and, hoping Melanie was watching, Linden took his arm and sailed into the drawing room.

Mason came towards them with a tray of cocktails and Randal took two glasses and handed one to Linden.

"Did you have any difficulty in getting the night off?" he asked.

"No – although I might be called out if there's a sudden rush."

"Let's hope there won't be." He raised his glass. "To an uninterrupted evening."

Linden sipped her cocktail and looked appreciatively about the handsome room. Some of the furniture had been removed and rugs had been taken from the parquet floor. Couches and extra chairs were set along the walls and a stereo deck was providing the music.

"People always seem reluctant to be first on the floor. Shall we start them off?" Randal said, smiling at her.

"If you like." She set down her glass and let him draw her to him. Over his shoulder she saw Melanie pausing in the doorway. She was accompanied by a short grey-haired man, presumably her father, and, as she caught sight of Randal and his partner, there was no mistaking the annoyance on her lovely imperious face.

Randal danced well, but Linden would not have cared if he had merely walked in time to the music. It was enough to be held in his arms.

Soon other people followed them on to the floor and he drew her closer.

"There's something different about you tonight," he said, suddenly looking down at her. "It's not just that dress. What's happened to you?"

"I'm in a party mood," she said lightly. "Do you disapprove? One can't be serious all the time."

"Naturally not," he said, dryly. "The mood is very becoming. What is your scent?"

"Oh – Balmain's 'Jolie Madame'."

"Very appropriate."

"You are complimentary tonight."

"I'm also in a party mood." He swung her into a turn. "I hope I didn't butt in on anything when I called the other night?"

She managed an enquiring look, then said carelessly, "Oh, when you brought my shoe back? No, of course not."

"I thought you looked slightly *distraite*."

"Did I? It had been a hectic day."

"Nice chap, Peter Carbury."

"Yes, isn't he?" Linden said casually.

The music ended and he released her. "Come and meet the Delaneys. I think you'll like them," he said, slipping a hand under her elbow.

The Delaneys were a couple of about the same age as Randal. Michael was a short thickset Irishman with a rugged humorous face and brilliant blue eyes. His wife was a tiny elfin creature, as fragile as he was sturdy.

"What have you been doing to yourself, Lisa?" Randal asked, when he had introduced them. Mrs. Delaney was wearing a white wristlet glove on her left hand and the first finger was swollen with bandages.

"She cut herself on a tin again," Michael informed him. "Considering that we live on canned food, you'd think she'd have learnt to handle them without always hacking herself." He leavened the gibe with a look of such indulgent tenderness that Linden knew they must be very happy together.

"Well, if you had a normal job, we wouldn't have so many tinned meals," Lisa Delaney said calmly. "Mike is a vet," she explained to Linden. "If you ever meet one – run! They make the most abominable husbands. Every time I cook a really lavish meal, Mike rings up to say he's calving a cow or giving a drench or something sordid."

"Do you live in the country, then?" Linden asked, laughing.

"Yes – miles from anywhere. Ghastly! I keep urging Mike to move to a town, but he has this passion for livestock, so what can one do?"

"You don't look so rustic," Randal remarked, grinning at her.

Anyone less like a country vet's wife was hard to imagine, Linden decided. Apart from her bandaged finger, Lisa Delaney was exquisitely groomed, and her white georgette dress was certainly not the creation of a village dressmaker.

"Randal, I adore you!" Lisa said happily. "This bucolic oaf reduces my morale to shreds by telling me my dress looks like a nightie, but one look from those bold black eyes of yours and my spirits are quite restored."

"Come and dance with me, then – if Mike doesn't mind?"

"You're welcome to her, old boy." Her husband waved them away, then turned to Linden. "She's a mad little creature, isn't she?"

"I think she's lovely," Linden said sincerely. "Was she an actress before you married?"

"That's clever of you," he said, smiling. "Though I suppose it's fairly obvious really. They're all slightly crazy in the theatre, aren't they?"

"I was guessing by her looks," Linden said. "She has such an expressive face."

"Yes, she was doing pretty well before I dragged her into the wilds. Mostly television and one or two film parts. She's really too small for the stage. I say, would you care to dance? I'm not very good at it, but I'll try not to ruin your shoes."

After dancing with Randal, whose chin was on a level with her forehead, Linden found it strange to be held by someone who was barely her own height. As he had admitted, Mike Delaney was not an accomplished dancer, but he was such a likeable person that she did not mind being steered round the floor in a series of darts and dashes.

The two couples rejoined each other at the end of the quick-step and Randal brought drinks. He and Mike began a discussion on cars – the Delaneys had just bought a new one – and Lisa turned to Linden.

"Randal told me about you when he came over to see us last week. I was expecting someone madly capable-looking," she said frankly. "Not that he described you as a gorgon, but I've been terrified of nurses ever since I had my appendix whipped out."

"Did they torture you?" Linden asked, laughing. She wondered how Randal *had* described her.

"Well, they didn't actually strap me to the table and fish it out with a buttonhook, but they had a mania for washing people at the most impossible hours. You know, shaking us awake at five o'clock in the morning and then tucking the bedclothes so tight we could hardly breathe."

"Yes, I know. I used to do it myself," Linden replied.

"Did you really? You look much too tender-hearted," Lisa said candidly.

Randal must have been listening to them, because he turned and said, "Don't you believe it. When she's in uniform, she has a heart of stone."

"I'm sure you could melt it if you tried, darling," Lisa said, with a mischievous glance.

Over her head, Randal gave Linden a long challenging look. "Perhaps I will," he said, turning back to Mike.

Lisa turned to study the other guests. "I see our tame siren is still on the warpath," she said, in a lower tone which the men would not hear. "Have you met her?"

Linden followed the direction in which she was looking and saw Melanie holding court to several young men. Now that the upper part of her body was no longer swathed in white fox furs, the whole of her dress was visible. Below the low décolletage, the emerald material appeared to have been pasted to her figure. Above it, a diamond and emerald necklace glittered on her golden skin.

"What do you mean, still on the warpath?" Linden asked quietly.

"Oh, heavens – don't you know? She's determined to capture Randal. And Ma Craig is equally in favour," she added wryly.

This last remark set the seal on Linden's liking for Lisa. Anyone who could dismiss the redoubtable Adela as 'Ma Craig' was well worth knowing.

"How do you know – that Melanie has designs?" she asked.

"Not from Randal. I don't think he has a clue – you know what men are. I spotted it one night when we came to dinner. I sometimes wonder if she might not pull it off. She has certain assets, and Randal has a pretty disenchanted attitude towards women, you know."

"Has he?" Linden said casually.

"Well, who wouldn't after growing up with Adela in command? That woman is enough to disillusion anyone. Mike's aunt used to live next door – her house has been pulled down now – and she told me that after Andrew was born, poor Randal never had a look in."

"What are you two muttering about?" her husband broke in.

"Just feminine chit-chat, darling. Much too frivolous

150

to interest the great male intellect," Lisa said gaily. "Oh, hello, Melanie."

Melanie stopped beside them, lovely and assured. From the warmth with which she greeted Lisa, one would have thought them close friends. Presently, as she had doubtless intended he should, Randal asked her to dance.

"I wonder?" Lisa said thoughtfully, watching them move away.

"Wonder what, pet?" Mike enquired.

"I wonder if Randal is immune, or if he's secretly affected. It's always so hard to tell his real reactions. Mike, if you were single again, would you be interested in her?"

Evidently Michael Delaney was accustomed to being asked such questions in public, and did not look at all embarrassed, but considered the matter for some seconds.

"Well, apart from the fact that you're the only glamorous piece that's ever looked at me twice – no!" he said definitely.

"Why not?" his wife demanded.

"Oh, she's fetching enough – very much so. I just don't care for the type."

"Do you think Randal might?"

Before he could reply the boy called John who had talked to Linden at the christening party came up and asked her to dance.

She did not see Randal again until the supper break, when she was talking to Paula and Andrew and he joined them.

"I must slip up and see that Jenny is all right. See you presently, Linden," Paula said, glancing at her expensive evening watch.

Presently, Andrew also excused himself, and Randal said, "It's getting hot in here. Would you like some fresh air?"

151

She knew by instinct that he expected her to demur.

"What a good idea," she said evenly.

They walked through the drawing room and out of the french windows on to the terrace.

Several other couples had had the same thought. There was a ghostly shimmer of moonlit white tulle under the beeches and the sheen of blue taffeta on the path to the rose garden.

"Let's go down to the lake," Randal said quietly. He had dropped his hand from her arm and they walked a little apart.

"I like the Delaneys very much," Linden said presently.

"I thought you would. I've known Mike for years. His aunt was a neighbour of ours when I was a boy, and he used to come to stay with her."

"How did he meet Lisa? They seem such an odd combination."

"At a wedding, I believe. Are you in favour of like pairing off with like?" Randal asked.

"Not particularly – but I should have thought she would feel a bit lost in a quiet market town."

"She probably does sometimes, but that flippant manner is only surface cover," Randal replied. "Basically she's the kind of woman who wants a man to be the centre of her world."

"That applies to most women, doesn't it?"

"Does it?" His tone was cynical. "A lot of them pick security. I would say a good percentage of women are more interested in their furniture or their children than in their husbands. Then they kick like hell if the poor chaps go off the rails."

"I didn't expect you to be an advocate of the 'world well lost for love' principle," she said, with a hint of raillery. "I thought you were one of the cold-blooded realists."

A patch of shadow hid the expression on his face,

but his voice was amused. "Remarks like that can be taken as a challenge."

They had reached the edge of the lake, and Linden was able to change the subject by admiring the Chinese lanterns.

"They were an idea of my mother's. The summer house was built for her, too."

"She was a singer, wasn't she?" Linden asked, as they began to walk along the path that skirted the water.

"Yes. She and my father were not unlike Mike and Lisa – at least, as far as dissimilarity of interests went. But my mother never really adjusted to life in Melchester. She'd been brought up on the Continent and never had a settled home. I think the narrowness of English provincial life must have seemed pretty futile to her."

"How old were you when she died?"

"About six. I don't really remember her very well, except as a kind of attractive feminine presence."

They came to the summer house and he took her hand to guide her up the steps. There was a wicker couch facing the doorway. Randal felt the cushions.

"They aren't damp, and I think they're reasonably clean," he said.

Linden sat down, her skirts billowing about her. She accepted a cigarette. In the flare of the lighter she saw that Randal was smiling. Then he snuffed the flame, and as a cloud momentarily obscured the moon, all she could see of him was the whiteness of his shirt, the glowing tip of his cigarette and the luminous face of his wristwatch.

She looked away towards the lights of the house and the movements of people on the lawn. Perhaps it was a trick of moonlight, but they looked very far away and unreal. From here, one could not even hear the music: only the whisper of the water-lily leaves and the croak of a frog in the reeds.

"Is it coming up to your expectations?" Randal said suddenly.

"The party? Why, yes, I—"

"No, the dangerous excitement of being out here alone with me."

The hardness of his tone was like a slap on the face. "What changed your mind? Was I too easily rebuffed the last time, or did you decide to prove you are the sophisticated type?"

"I don't know what you're talking about," Linden said bewilderedly.

"You didn't suspect that I might have brought you out here to make a pass at you?"

As the implication sank in, Linden went stiff with anger. She would have sprung to her feet, but he grasped her wrist and held her where she was.

"Don't panic," he said silkily. "You're in a party mood – remember? It's not much of a party that doesn't include a romantic interlude by moonlight."

"Let me go! You ... you're disgusting!" she said violently.

"You didn't seem to think so ten minutes ago."

It was useless to struggle. His fingers were bruisingly strong. She forced herself to sit still.

"Ten minutes ago you weren't being so utterly insufferable," she said, through set teeth.

He laughed in a way that made her shiver.

"Randal, please ..."

Her appeal was stifled as he pulled her into his arms and found her mouth. Afterwards, even thinking of that kiss, Linden would chill with shame. At one moment she was loathing and despising him, and an instant later she was yielding to delight, all her resistance fled.

At last, when she was trembling and dazed and breathless, he let her go. She sank against the cushions, her senses spinning. She was conscious of nothing but a kind of dreamlike wonder that a kiss could be such heaven. Randal's hands slipped up her arms to her smooth bare shoulders and he bent towards her. "Linden ..."

His voice shattered the spell. As swiftly as she had been caught in that wild excitement, she woke to reality. A rush of self-revulsion at the ease with which she succumbed swept over her.

"Don't touch me!" With her whole healthy young strength she pushed him away from her and somehow scrambled to her feet. Then, grabbing a handful of organza, too upset to care if her lovely dress was torn by the brambles near the path, she ran blindly round the lake and up the steps to the lawn.

Fortunately all the strollers had gone back into the house, so no one saw her flight. A hasty glance over her shoulder showed no sign of Randal in pursuit, but realising that she could not go indoors until she had recovered some measure of composure, she hid in the shadow of the beeches and waited to recover her breath.

Presently, remembering the passage through which she had once wheeled the pram, she managed to get upstairs without attracting attention. There were several women in the bedroom, but they were all too busy gossiping to take any notice of her and the adjoining bathroom was empty.

It was only then that she discovered she had not got her evening bag. It must be on the couch in the summer house. She would have to slip out and recover it – unless Randal brought it back with him.

There was a rustle of skirts outside the door and a girl in blue came in. Linden turned on the taps and began to wash her hands. She managed to give the girl a forced smile.

"Heavenly party, isn't it? I always adore coming here," the girl said effusively.

"Yes, marvellous," Linden agreed hollowly. "I – I

wonder if you could possibly lend me some lipstick. I stupidly forgot to bring any."

The girl lookèd faintly disapproving, but she passed over a gilt case and began to powder her nose. Linden took a tissue from the box on the toilet shelf, scrubbed her lips clean and retouched them.

"Thanks very much," she said politely.

"I say, look at your wrist. Have you knocked it on something?"

Linden raised her forearm. A series of reddened imprints marked the skin just about the joint.

The girl giggled. "You have picked a he-man!" she said vulgarly.

Linden gave her a freezing glare and stalked back to the bedroom. At first she had intended to leave immediately. If any of the family noticed her early departure, let Randal explain her reasons! But now that her bag was mislaid, she would have to wait. If she left now and Randal had it, he was quite capable of following her to the flat. If he hadn't, it would tarnish in the damp.

But the thought of going back to the summer house was repugnant. Perhaps she could ask young John Conyers to have a look for her.

Still feeling profoundly disturbed, she mustered all her self-control and walked downstairs.

"Hello, Nurse Templar. We haven't had our dance," said Andrew Craig, meeting her in the hall.

She let him take her into the drawing room, quickly skimming the room to see if Randal had returned.

"Sorry. My fault," Andrew said politely, as she missed a step. Had Linden been in the mood to be amused, she would have noticed that he danced rather as if he were driving a sports car – spinning into turns and cutting through narrow gaps with a practised but daring eye. As it was, she had to concentrate on following him and was glad when the record finished.

"Thank you. Can I get you a drink? Oh, look, I think Mrs. Delaney is waving to you."

Lisa was in the hall. Linden excused herself to Andrew and went to her.

"We're leaving. Our baby-sitter can't stay after twelve and it's half an hour's drive," Lisa said, slipping her arms into the sleeves of a crimson silk coat which her husband was holding for her.

"I didn't know you had a baby."

"We haven't. I'm coping with my sister's nine-year-old for a couple of weeks. Look, what I wanted to say is will you come out to supper with us one evening? I know you're pretty busy, but Randal can fix the day. It'll only be pot luck, so we don't need any notice. Oh, here is Randal."

Linden kept her eyes on Lisa and willed herself not to betray any reaction.

"I was suggesting that you two should come and sup with us, Randal, but perhaps Sunday lunch would suit Linden better. Anyway, you fix it up with her and give me a tinkle," Lisa suggested. "Oh dear, I wish we didn't have to rush away, but we swore to Mrs. Hotblack that we wouldn't be a second later than midnight."

When they had gone Randal said, "This is yours, isn't it?" He held out the silver kid bag.

"Thank you." She took it without looking at him, and turned quickly away.

"Linden, I want to talk to you," he said urgently.

"There's nothing to say," she said woodenly. "And I shan't be going to the Delaneys'."

"Now listen—"

"I don't want to listen, Mr. Craig," she said cuttingly. "Will you please leave me alone?" And, still without meeting his eyes, she hurried back into the drawing room, looking desperately about for John.

The young man was chatting to another youth. He brightened when he saw her approaching him.

"I was looking for you earlier, but you seemed to have disappeared," he said.

"John – have you got a car here?"

He nodded. "What's the matter?"

"Don't look so alarmed." She managed a smile. "It's just that ... that I've got rather a headache. If I ask for a taxi it will cause a fuss. Could you be a dear and run me home?"

"Oh, what bad luck! Of course I'll take you – but are you sure you wouldn't feel O.K. if you had a couple of aspirins or something?"

"No, I'd really rather go, and I have to be up early tomorrow."

"Can I get your coat?"

"I brought it down just now. It's in the hall. I – I won't stop to say any goodbyes now. I'll telephone Mrs. Craig tomorrow."

"Well, look, I'll get it for you and then we'll stroll out by way of the windows. Then nobody will notice," he suggested.

"Bless you. It's a white silk shawl on the chair by the telephone table."

He was gone only a few moments, but Linden fretted with impatience in case Randal saw that she was alone and forced her to talk to him. Only when the car was sweeping down the drive did she breathe a long sigh of relief.

"I hope you didn't mind my asking you to help me?" she said apologetically, as they passed through the gateway.

"Good lord, no. I'm delighted. I say – I hope you won't be annoyed – but I've got a bit of a confession to make."

"I know. You hadn't met me before the christening," she said dryly.

"I was afraid you'd seen through it," he said ruefully. "I don't really know why I pretended – except that I

158

wanted to talk to you. If I'd waited for a formal introduction the whole thing would probably have been over."

"I didn't mind."

"It must have seemed rather clottish."

Her laugh had a brittle note. "Aren't we all 'clottish' sometimes?" she said wryly.

"I'm sure *you* aren't," he said seriously. "You looked marvellous tonight: knocked all the other women into a cocked hat."

The earnest gallantry made Linden want to weep. She thought that, when John was older, he would probably be rather like Peter. Kind and dependable and sincere. Never wildly exciting perhaps – but never harsh or mocking or ruthless. Never like Randal Craig.

When Linden woke up next morning, she really did have a headache. As she drew the curtains, the bright sunlight made her wince and shield her eyes.

Dragging herself into the bathroom, she swallowed a couple of aspirins, cleaned her teeth and splashed her face with cold water.

The telephone started to ring and she groaned. It was barely half-past seven, and it must have been nearly two when she got to sleep. The thought of the day's work appalled her.

"Linden? Jill here. Did you have a good time?" Jill's voice sounded almost indecently bright and clear.

"I don't know. I'm still half asleep," Linden said shortly.

"Well, sorry to drag you out of bed, but I thought I'd better warn you. There's been a bit of a flap on."

Linden smothered a yawn. "What sort of a flap?" she asked tiredly.

"An avalanche of infants," Jill said cheerfully. "I've just come off duty – and so has everyone else, from what I can make of it. Even Mrs. Langley was out."

She sounded light-hearted, but Linden felt a sudden stab of disquiet.

"What did you mean – warn me?" she asked quickly.

"Now don't panic, but I looked in at the clinic on my way home and it seems they tried to get hold of you last night and couldn't. You may be mildly unpopular in certain quarters."

"Why couldn't they get hold of me? They knew where I was," Linden said sharply.

"I don't know any details. I just thought I'd tip you off. It'll give you a chance to think of a reasonable alibi."

"I don't need an alibi. You knew I was at the Craigs'. So did Mrs. Langley. Why didn't they phone me there?" Linden demanded.

"I gathered that they had. Look, there's no need to worry about it. They must have made a mistake. In the rush of calls, it isn't very surprising. What riled me was that, after toiling all yesterday afternoon, I'd hardly had time to swallow my tea and bath before I was out again. That silly Mrs. Brown was two days overdue, so she swallowed about half a bottle of castor oil and nearly did herself in. Honestly, the idiocy of . . ."

"I'd better get down to the clinic and sort this thing out," Linden cut in. "Thanks for letting me know, Jill. I expect I'll see you later. 'Bye."

Putting down the receiver, she stood biting her knuckles for some moments. She was mystified and a good deal worried by what Jill had told her.

After a quick breakfast, she set out for the clinic. One of the pupil midwives was passing through the hall when she arrived, and she asked if Mrs. Langley was about.

"Yes, she is in her office, I think," the girl said, smiling. She was a plump little Nigerian with large child-like dark eyes and the most beautiful white teeth.

Linden tapped on the door of Mrs. Langley's room

and was bidden to enter. The Non-Medical Supervisor was sitting at her desk, writing a report. As usual, she looked calm and competent in her spotless white coat.

"Good morning, Nurse Templar," she said quietly, putting down her pen. But today her pleasant smile was absent.

"Good morning." Linden found that she was absurdly nervous. Although she had not, to her knowledge, done anything wrong, there was something in Mrs. Langley's expression that made her uneasy. "I – I've been told that I was wanted last night and couldn't be found," she stammered.

"Sit down, Nurse." Mrs. Langley blotted the form she had been filling and put it in a file. Then she rested her elbows on the arms of her chair, folded her hands and gave Linden a long considering look.

"When you explained that you had been asked to a dance on what would not ordinarily have been one of your free evenings, I agreed to the proposal on the understanding that you could be called if necessary," she said, quietly. "It seemed unlikely that your enjoyment would be interrupted, but as it turned out, we were extremely rushed last night. The entire duty staff was working and I had to go out myself. I was just about to leave when a call came from one of your patients. I rang the number you gave me and was told that you were not there. I then rang your own number, but there was no reply. I made another call ten minutes later and there was still no answer. Finally, I had to get Nurse Fisher, who had already been to two cases in the previous twenty-four hours."

Linden bit her lip. If she had not been at the Craigs' when Mrs. Langley telephoned them, then she must have been on her way home with John. But the drive couldn't possibly have taken more than six or seven minutes at the very most, so she was certain to have heard the second call.

"I can't understand it," she said blankly, explaining this to the supervisor. "What time did you call the Craigs?"

"It must have been about ten-fifteen."

"But I was still there then," Linden exclaimed hopefully. "They had a buffet supper at half-past nine and then afterwards..." She broke off abruptly, a vivid flush colouring her pale cheeks.

"And then?" Mrs. Langley prompted.

Linden swallowed. "Then I went for a stroll in the gardens," she said flatly. "I was outside for about ten minutes, perhaps a quarter of an hour. But several people saw me leave the house and they had no reason to think I'd gone altogether. Why, about half the other guests were walking outside for a while after supper." Mrs. Langley's face showed no reaction, and Linden said anxiously, "You do believe me, don't you?"

There was a pause before the older woman replied. Then she said quietly, "Nurses are only human and they have their faults like everyone else. But I've never yet met a C.S.M. who didn't take her job seriously or who failed the peculiar responsibility of this work. Yes, I believe you, Nurse Templar. But I should like to find out why my message didn't reach you."

"So should I," Linden said seriously. "Which of my patients was it? And what happened?"

"It was Mrs. Rice, and, fortunately for Nurse Fisher, it was a false alarm."

"I thought it sounded odd. She isn't due to have her baby for another three weeks and everything seemed in order when I checked her on Tuesday."

"She had evidently eaten something to upset her and misjudged the effects," Mrs. Langley said, with a smile.

"Who did you speak to on the telephone?" Linden asked. "The maid usually answers it and she knows me well."

162

"It wasn't the maid. It was a man. He said he would see if he could find you, and then a few moments later he told me that you had left."

"A man," Linden murmured, puzzled.

The telephone rang and Mrs. Langley answered it. "Will you hold on a moment, please." She covered the mouthpiece with her hand and said to Linden, "We'll leave it for the present, Nurse. I hope you'll believe me when I say that I felt sure that there was a sound explanation."

"Thank you, Mrs. Langley." Linden returned her smile and left the room.

The door of the staff dining room was open and she went in to see if there was some tea going. Two of the resident nurses were still having breakfast, and, from their good-natured banter, it was evident that they had heard the gist of the incident.

Linden took their chaffing in good part, but her mind was preoccupied with what Mrs. Langley had told her. Who could have answered the telephone at the Craig house last night? One of the guests who happened to be near when it rang and who did not appreciate the urgency of the call? But surely Mrs. Langley must have made that clear. Perhaps the man had been mildly tight and thought he was doing Linden a favour. But she hadn't noticed anyone who looked as if they might have had too many drinks. It had not been that sort of party.

Suddenly a dreadful possibility occurred to her. It was so unpleasant that, almost at once, she put it aside as being too horrible to consider.

But she must have shown what she had thought, as Nurse Miles said quickly, "Don't look so downhearted, Templar. We're only having you on."

Linden stared at her blankly for a moment. She forced a smile. "Yes, I know," she said hastily.

"How did you get on anyway?" Nurse Lacey asked,

with interest. "Tell us all about it. Some people" – she winked at Nurse Miles – "never get a chance to fraternize with the nobs. Was it madly posh?"

Linden swallowed the rest of her tea. "I can't stop now, I've got a heavy morning. I'll tell you about it later."

But, as the day wore on, that shaming explanation nagged at the back of her mind. Even after what had happened in the summer house, she shrank from giving it credence. Yet . . . it *could* be the answer.

At lunch time, Jill looked in. "Are you in the doghouse, or has everything blown over?" she asked.

Linden tried to sound light-hearted as she said she wasn't expecting an official reprimand for the time being.

"On a diet?" Jill asked lightly, noting the cup of coffee and piece of cold toast which appeared to be her friend's lunch.

"I'm not very hungry. Can I get you something, or are you going home?"

"I wouldn't mind a sandwich I'm ravenous, but I haven't got time for much," said Jill, glancing at her watch.

Linden cut her a thick ham sandwich and heated some more milk. She was afraid that Jill would also want to know about the party and was reluctant to discuss it. If it had been possible, she would have liked to expunge the whole evening from her mind.

Jill had just left and Linden was washing her hands when the telephone rang. It was Paula Craig.

"I was so sorry to hear you didn't feel well last night. John told us he took you home. Are you feeling better?" she asked concernedly.

"Yes, much, thank you. I – I hope you didn't think me very rude, but I didn't want to spoil your evening. It was a very nice party," Linden answered awkwardly.

"I'm glad you enjoyed the first part anyway," Paula

said warmly. "Everyone admired your blissful dress and wanted to know who you were." She laughed. "I think John Conyers has rather lost his heart to you. I hope he won't be a nuisance. Boys of that age take themselves so seriously."

"Mrs. Craig ... you didn't hear anyone mention a call for me during the evening, did you?" Linden said, on impulse.

"Look, do call me Paula, won't you? It seems silly to be formal now we're friends. No, I don't think there was a call for you. Were you expecting one?"

"No – I just wondered if there had been," Linden explained.

"As far as I know there weren't any calls last night," Paula said, sounding rather puzzled. "Oh ... wait a minute. Yes, I saw Randal at the telephone once. But it couldn't have been for you or he would have told you, wouldn't he?"

"Do you remember what time that was?" Linden found her voice was not quite steady.

"Heavens, I haven't a clue." There was a slight pause while Paula thought about it. "It was after supper," she decided. "I remember he looked rather cross about something. Look, I'll ask him when he comes in and ring you back."

"Oh, no, please – it isn't important," Linden said quickly. "Don't say anything about it. I must go now, I'm afraid. Thank you again for having me. Goodbye."

She rang off, feeling strangely chilled. So the man who had answered the phone *had* been Randal, and Paula remembered that he had looked angry. But angry enough to take such a mean, cheap revenge for being repulsed? So angry that he could deliberately ignore the plight of whoever had needed Linden's help?

Even discounting his own connection with the clinic, it seemed a fantastic thing to have done.

"I can't believe it. *I can't!*" she whispered aloud.

Randal might be arrogant and hard, but he wasn't irresponsible. He wasn't a vindictive man. Surely he wasn't?

Yet what else was there to believe? All the evidence was against him.

If I really loved him, I would trust him in spite of the evidence, she thought achingly. But I don't love him. It was just an overpowering attraction, a counterfeit of love.

When she got home that night, Peter was waiting for her.

"I've got to talk to you, Linden," he said, without preamble.

She was too exhausted to argue, or to worry what her neighbours might be thinking if they had seen him hovering on the landing. Barely glancing at him, she unlocked the door and let him follow her in.

"You look ghastly," he said flatly, as she slumped into a chair and pulled off her hat.

"I feel it," Linden said bitterly. She began to laugh.

"Stop it," he said sharply.

"It's all right. I'm not going to have hysterics," she said mildly. "I was just trying out a theory I read. According to this article, laughter is the cure for all our troubles. A few hearty guffaws and one feels on top of the world." She closed her eyes and leaned her head against the back of the chair. "I don't think it's frightfully successful."

Peter laid his hand on her forehead for a second, thrust a thermometer into her mouth and felt her pulse. She couldn't be bothered to protest.

"You need a good meal and an early night," he said, shaking the mercury down. "I'll make a pot of tea."

Linden watched him disappear into the kitchen and heard the hiss of the gas jets and the rattle of the caddy. She knew that she ought to jump up and tell him not to fuss, but she felt so drained of energy that it was too much trouble even to change her shoes. She had never felt like this before. All her emotions seemed suddenly to have dried up so that nothing was of any importance. It was like being suspended in a vacuum, watching the world go by but taking no interest in it.

I would feel better if I could weep and wail and grind my teeth, she thought with odd detachment.

Peter came back with the tea. He had made a plate of toast and seemed to have spread her entire week's supply of butter on it.

"I met Nurse Adams. She said she thought you looked a bit off colour," he said, pouring the tea.

"She should mind her own business," Linden said, without rancour. "I'm not a ten-year-old."

Peter said nothing. When she had eaten the toast, he lit a cigarette and handed it to her.

"I don't know why you're treating me like an invalid. I'm perfectly well, you know," Linden said, sipping the hot sweet tea.

He filled his pipe. "What happened last night, Linden? Nurse Adams told me about this telephone business, but I think there's more to it than that. You aren't the type to be shattered by that kind of mix-up."

"Am I shattered?" she said carelessly.

"You can't bottle it up indefinitely."

The vacuum seemed to have a chink. The way he was watching her began to irritate.

"Are you thinking of setting up as a psychiatrist?" she said coldly. "I don't think you'd find my sub-conscious particularly interesting."

He put the pipe on the table and leaned forward to take her hands. "Linden . . . darling—"

She snatched them away. "Oh, Peter, stop being so kind to me!" Her voice broke and she twisted away from him to hide her anguished face.

"I'm not being kind, you little fool. I love you," he said violently.

The next moment he was kneeling beside her and her face was buried in his shoulder.

Some time later, Linden fumbled for the handkerchief in his breast pocket. "Oh, lord! What an exhibition," she said, in a muffled voice.

Peter took the handkerchief and blotted her wet cheeks. His tenderness made her eyes fill with tears again.

"Come on, buck up," he said gently. "It's over now, sweetheart. Everyone makes mistakes."

"But—"

"I'd better ring up home in case there are any calls for me," he said swiftly, cutting her short. "You go and powder your nose and then I'll show you what an excellent cook I am. Got any spaghetti in the larder?"

"I think so. But, Peter, I don't—"

"Do as you're told." He pushed her towards the bathroom and turned to the telephone.

He stayed until nine, helping to wash up the astonishing number of utensils which had apparently been necessary to his culinary efforts, and then lounging on the couch and talking with almost non-stop cheerfulness about anything and everything. It was not until he was on the point of leaving that he dropped his determined jocularity and was suddenly serious.

"Promise you'll go to bed now and try to sleep," he said gravely. "It's always a waste of time to mull over one's bad patches."

"Yes, I'll try," she agreed. "And thank you so much, Peter."

"You don't have to thank me," he said roughly. "I want you to be happy, my sweet. Goodnight. Sleep tight." And, bending, he kissed her cheek, and then was gone.

The following morning, Linden had a letter from her mother.

Dearest Linden, (Mrs. Templar had written)

You will be surprised to hear that Louise is engaged —to a Scots farmer! As you can imagine, Daddy and I were completely stunned. We knew nothing about it until she brought him home and announced the news. His name is Malcolm Ferguson and he seems charming—although quite different from L's usual run. I gather that he is a Master or Laird or something impressive, and the farm is very up-to-date and prosperous. For a moment I had awful visions of Louise being carried off to some derelict crofter's hut. Even so, she must be very much in love with him to consider leaving London and going into tweeds and serviceable shoes. I did ring up yesterday to tell you the news, but there was no reply. I hope you aren't working too hard, darling. You will be coming home on your next free weekend, I hope. It seems so long since we saw you.

The letter ran to four pages, mainly about Louise and her fiancé and the plans for the wedding. Linden read it twice. She was glad that her sister had found happiness and liked the sound of Malcolm Ferguson. But she couldn't help thinking that there was a good deal of irony in the fact that Louise had finally succumbed to a rugged countryman while she, Linden, had badly bruised her heart in quite another direction.

On the way past the post office, she despatched a congratulatory telegram. The news from home had distracted her from her own concerns and she was too busy during the day to have time to brood.

It was four o'clock when she went home and she was almost at the entrance to the flats before she recognised the car by the curb. For a moment, she almost swung the bike into a turn and headed for the clinic. Then she realised that she had to go home eventually, and Randal might wait there all evening if he were determined to see her. Considering the circumstances, his effrontery astounded her.

"What do you want?" she asked coldly, as he got out of the car and came towards her.

He had the audacity to smile at her. "Are you determined to be angry with me?" he asked, with a wry face.

"I'm not so much angry as aghast," she said flatly. "I thought you had some pretensions to decency."

"Decency?" His eyebrows shot up. "That's coming it rather strong, isn't it?"

"Perhaps it depends how you look at it," she said scathingly.

"I certainly don't regard a kiss as something indecent. You're not a Victorian miss."

"I wasn't referring to that – I'm doing my best to forget about it," Linden retorted icily.

"Then what the devil are you referring to?"

"I don't want to discuss it. Will you please leave me alone?" she said, with controlled fury.

Randal looked at her intently. Then he shrugged and said, "All right. If that's how you feel, there's not much I can do about it. But I think you'll change your mind." He half turned away, then stopped and said, "Incidentally, Paula mentioned your call yesterday and said you sounded worried, so I checked the matter. There was a message for you during the evening, but it was taken by the waiter from the catering firm and, for reasons which are rather complicated, it went astray. I realised it must have put you in a spot, so I rang Mrs. Langley and explained the matter."

"The waiter?" Linden said dully. "You mean it wasn't—" She stopped abruptly, her eyes widening with distress.

Randal stared at her, his brows drawing together. "I see," he said finally. "So you thought I was responsible. You certainly have a very high opinion of my morals."

"You don't understand," she stammered.

"You were right," he said harshly. "It seems that what happened in the garden was a mistake on all counts."

And, before she could find words to stop him, he swung back into the car, slammed the door and drove off.

CHAPTER SEVEN

THE next day was Sunday. Linden finished her morning calls by noon and then, rather than go back to the flat before one, she looked in on Mrs. Cowley, whose baby was now eight days later than expected.

Margaret Cowley was vigorously wielding a vacuum cleaner as she passed the sitting-room window. She switched it off and came into the hall as Linden stepped through the open front door.

"Hello, Nurse. Still nothing doing. I'm beginning to wonder if this infant will ever budge."

"He obviously takes after you," Linden said, laughing. Mrs. Cowley always arrived at classes ten minutes after time, breathlessly apologetic but congenitally unpunctual.

"I made Jim go fishing. I thought if he wasn't around to rush out and phone you, it might work the oracle," she said hopefully.

Linden stayed for half an hour, then went home for lunch.

As she climbed the stairs to her landing, she was surprised to see a couple outside her door. They were deeply absorbed in kissing each other. It wasn't until she coughed and they drew apart that she recognised her sister.

"Louise! What are you doing here?" Linden exclaimed, glancing at the tall grey-eyed stranger who was sheepishly wiping a smudge of lipstick from his chin.

"I hope you're not tearing off to deliver quads, darling. We've come for lunch. Mother thought it would be a nice surprise for you. Oh, this is Malcolm, by the way."

"So I gathered," Linden replied with a twinkle.

Malcolm held out his hand and took hers in a firm clasp. "I hope we aren't going to be a nuisance," he said, with a friendly smile.

"No, of course not. Come in. Fortunately it's a fairly slack day. I'm afraid I can't offer you a very lavish lunch, but I'm awfully glad you came."

"Oh, that's all right, sweetie. We brought lunch with us," Louise said, indicating a box on the floor. "Cold chicken salad and a bottle of champagne – though I suppose you daren't drink too much in case you're summoned to a case."

They all trooped into the flat and Linden laid the table while Louise and her fiancé unpacked the box.

"Is that your car outside? You must have got up very early," Linden remarked.

"We did. I'm getting into training for the rigours of being a farmer's wife. Oh, damn – don't say you've got to run." This as the door bell rang.

Linden answered it and found Peter outside.

"Hello," he said, smiling. "Mother's gone out for the day, so I thought I'd come round and see if I could scrounge a spot of lunch."

"Come in."

Peter heard Malcolm speaking to Louise and his smile faded. Linden knew what he thought. Malcolm's deep, quiet voice was very like Randal's. It had already given her a quick lance of pain.

"Come in. It's my sister and her fiancé. They've brought a picnic lunch and I'm sure there's ample for four," she said hurriedly.

"No, really, I won't butt in. I . . ."

"Don't be silly." Linden took his sleeve and pulled him into the room.

After the introductions, Peter continued to protest

that he didn't want to gatecrash a family reunion, but they quickly stifled his arguments.

After lunch, the two men volunteered to wash up, and Linden and Louise relaxed on the sofa.

"You've changed so much," Linden said wonderingly, as they lit cigarettes.

It was not only the alteration in her sister's appearance that she had noticed, although Louise was wearing less make-up and a pearly pink nail varnish instead of her usual crimson lacquer. But as well as these superficial differences, her whole manner seemed to have softened and become warmer. Instead of being blasée and cool, she was suddenly animated and gay.

"No, I haven't, sweetie," Louise said wryly. "I've just dropped the pose, that's all. I don't need it any longer. More coffee?"

Linden nodded, and Louise shared the remainder between them. "I don't suppose you remember – you were in your first year at St. Peter's and poring over textbooks – but I had quite a whirl with a man called Jordan Forbes," she said.

"Yes, I do. He was something in the theatre, wasn't he?"

"A producer. He's gone over to films in America now."

She watched a tendril of smoke drift upwards from the tip of her cigarette. "I took rather a bad knock over Jordan," she said, reflectively. "I must have been terribly innocent for my age. When I found out he had a wife in the background and that I was just one of several girls he was running around with on the side – well, it knocked the bottom out of my life for a time."

"No one would ever have guessed," Linden put in.

"If they had it would have been the ultimate humiliation," Louise said. She shrugged. "I got over it eventually, but I was determined that it wouldn't happen again. I suppose I had some crazy idea of revenging myself on the whole male sex. Anyway, I skipped about ten years of normal development and patterned myself on one of these super-sophisticated witches of around thirty – no illusions, no heart, no nothing. If Malcolm hadn't come along, the shell would probably have become permanent."

"I like him so much. I'm sure you'll be terribly happy," Linden said sincerely.

"So do I – although Mother's still a bit dubious," Louise replied lightly. "I haven't told her all this rigmarole and she can't see me settling in the country. But enough of me. What about your love-life?"

"I'm too busy with my job to have time for anything else," Linden said evasively.

"Are you?" Louise looked amused. "Too busy to have noticed that Peter is crazy about you?"

Linden looked anxiously towards the kitchen door, but it was safely shut.

"I should have thought he was just your type," Louise remarked.

"I suppose he is," Linden said, frowning. She got up and took a restless turn about the room. "Oh, Lou, I've been such a fool," she blurted out suddenly.

"That makes two of us, sweetie. What kind of a fool have you been?"

It was a long time since the sisters had confided in each other – not since Louise had been embroiled with Jordan Forbes, Linden realised – but suddenly the comfortable intimacy of their teens seemed to have been re-established. Shyly, but without awkwardness, she gave a résumé of her encounters with Randal.

"The trouble is that I'm not used to dealing with that type of man," she concluded. "I don't understand how they look at life."

"I was in the same sort of muddle over Malcolm at first," Louise admitted. "I was still playing the good time girl when I met him and I thought he'd hate the sight of me. I think if you're in love with any kind of man, you just have to grab all your chances and hope to heaven he's interested. The trouble with being a woman is that you can only play your hunches. There's no way of being sure until he suddenly drops on one knee – or leaves you flat!" she added, with a grimace.

"I suppose not," Linden agreed gloomily.

They were prevented from discussing the subject at length by the reappearance of the men, and at three o'clock Linden had a call from Mrs. Cowley's neighbour.

"I'll have to go, I'm afraid," she said regretfully.

"We'd have had to start back soon anyway," Louise said, stirring herself.

Linden said goodbye and left them to see themselves off. Peter accompanied her down to the courtyard.

"I'll look in this evening, if I may," he said, handing over her bag.

"I should think I'll be out till fairly late," Linden said.

"I'll call anyway. I like your sister and Ferguson, but I'd rather have you to myself," he said gently.

The Cowley baby was being true to maternal form. It was making up for its lateness by hustling into the world as fast as it could.

"I had a slight backache this morning, but I thought it was just an ordinary one," Mrs. Cowley explained, looking very pleased with herself.

Linden left her in the care of her neighbour and hurried back to fetch the gas-and-air machine, notify the clinic of her whereabouts and inform the Cowleys' doctor.

It was after ten when Linden got home that night and there was a note from Peter on the mat. He had been round at nine o'clock, but found her still out. Would she let him know if she was free the following evening? He expected to be free by half-past eight.

A little after eight the next night, Linden went round to Peter's surgery. She was still in uniform and his secretary assumed that the call was a professional one.

"Dr. Carbury is just seeing the last patient, Nurse. I don't think he'll be very long," she said, tidying her desk. "We only had eleven in tonight. Evening surgeries are always slack at this time of year. But once the autumn sets in they'll be packing in again. Half of them seem to treat the waiting room as a kind of club."

"I suppose it is for some of them," Linden suggested.

Mrs. Carbury had told her that several of the pensioners to whom she delivered meals looked forward to a visit to the doctor with pathetic eagerness. The warmth – in winter – of the waiting room, the interest of watching the patients come and go and the possibility of a chat with the next person in line – these things were a real treat when one lived in a single room, no longer of interest to anyone.

"Possibly. But they might consider the doctor," Miss Day said acidly. "I tell him he ought not to encourage them. Some of them come here when there's nothing in the least wrong with them. Dr. Carbury is much too soft-hearted."

At this point the patient emerged from the surgery and Miss Day whisked in to get Peter's signature on some letters she had typed. She came out a few minutes later looking slightly pink. Linden remembered Peter telling her that his secretary was a middle-aged dragon of awesome efficiency.

She's also hopelessly in love with him, she thought, with a flash of compassion.

"You may go in now, Nurse," Miss Day said briskly, slipping the letters in their envelopes. The strip lighting gave her complexion an unbecoming mottled blue tinge and accentuated the faint moustache on her upper lip.

Linden wondered what lay behind her militant attitude to life. A girlhood sacrificed to invalid parents perhaps, or merely the fact of being born a generation before cosmetics were a ladylike means of improving a plain face.

"Lord, what an evening!" Peter said wryly, after his first eager smile. He shrugged out of his jacket, lit a pipe and tilted back his chair, resting his feet on an open drawer of the desk.

"Varicose veins, piles, acne and an ingrowing toenail – some of the most dismal ailments to which man is heir." He tossed the matchstalk into the waste paper basket. "It's a far cry from aspirations of one's student days, isn't it?"

"You're tired," Linden said gently. "You know you wouldn't change if you could."

He shrugged. "Maybe – maybe not. Come into the house. Mother is out, but the fridge is always full. I wanted to take you for a run, but I'm taking Austin's calls as well as my own."

Linden hesitated. Seeing him in this mood of unwonted depression, she wondered if she ought not to say what she had intended. But every day's delay must make it more difficult.

"I mustn't stop. I'm all behind with the housework," she said quickly.

"Won't it ride for one more evening?"

"Peter ..." She rose and moved to the window, staring at the pattern of the frosted glass. "Peter, I don't think we ought to meet any more," she said, with decision.

She had expected him to protest, but he didn't speak until she turned to face him.

Then he said quietly, "I thought you'd changed your mind about ... the other thing."

"I have ... that is ... there was never anything to be changed."

His pipe had gone out. He reached for the matches again but did not strike one.

"You mean that, even if nothing else had cropped up, I still wouldn't stand a chance, is that it?"

Linden's throat was tight and tears pricked her eyelids. "I'm sorry, Peter," she whispered.

"Don't look so tragic, my dear. It isn't the end of the world." His smile was almost more than she could bear. "I'm not the type to languish for the rest of my life. Look, I don't want to labour this, but ... are you quite sure you've had enough time to get things straight?"

She gave a mute nod. "You're such a nice person, Peter. I - I couldn't go on taking your friendship without being honest," she said, very low.

He pushed the drawer into place and got slowly to his feet. She thought he looked ten years older.

"I'd better go," she said miserably.

He followed her into the passage and unlatched the outer door. "I'm afraid we're bound to meet each other professionally," he said. "I wish you wouldn't look so unhappy, my dear."

The tears blurred her eyes and she couldn't speak. There was nothing else to say. With a choked goodnight, she slipped past him and ran down the drive.

"I hear Melanie Fletcher has gone on a cruise to Jamaica," Jill remarked a few days later.

Linden rinsed out a specimen glass. They were in the examination room at the clinic, preparing for the Tuesday ante-natal session.

"How do you know?" she asked.

"Joanna told me." Joanna was Jill's younger sister who worked in the dress department of the town's largest store. "Melanie went in for a fitting on Saturday and Joanna heard her telling the buyer. Lucky thing! She's had one holiday already this year. I wonder how much a cruise like that would cost?"

"I don't know," Linden said absently. The information puzzled her, as Melanie had made no mention of the cruise at Paula's birthday party. It seemed odd, too, that she should go away for several weeks if she had designs on Randal. Unless it was in the hope that an absence would enhance his feelings towards her.

The week dragged by and Linden grew more and more restless and edgy. Minor irritations had suddenly become major catastrophes. On Friday, finding herself on the verge of tears merely because she had broken a favourite china ornament, she knew that she must get a grip on herself. She wished now that she lived with the other nurses at the clinic. Their company would have made it easier to forget the ache inside her, whereas, living out, it was only when she was working that she could forget herself.

On Saturday night she met Peter again. As she heard her patient's husband letting him into the house, she resented the circumstances which made it necessary for them to work together. But Peter gave no sign that her presence was an embarrassment to him, and soon they were both too busy to be conscious of their personal relationship.

Linden battled with her unrest for two weeks before she came to the decision that had lurked at the back of her mind since the last time she had seen Randal. She had tried to convince herself that her depressed state of mind could not last indefinitely. Then, one Saturday morning, she was shopping in the centre of the town when she saw him coming out of a bank.

If she had not been looking straight ahead, she would have walked into him. As it was, she was able to dodge into an arcade until his car had disappeared. The brief glimpse of his tall, broad-shouldered figure proved to her how futile it was to try and fight her emotions. Given time, she could forget him – she must! But not while she stayed in Melchester.

On Monday she went to Mrs. Langley and told her that she wanted to leave.

"To leave?" Mrs. Langley repeated, looking astonished. "But you have only been here for a few months."

"I know, but I'm afraid I must go," Linden said bleakly.

"May I know your reason?"

"It's nothing to do with the job – it's a personal matter."

"I see." Mrs. Langley studied her blotter for some moments. Then she said quietly, "I take it you have thought this over, Nurse Templar? Even with the present shortage of midwives in most parts of the country, I don't think this step is very wise. It might give the impression that you are unreliable."

"Yes, I realise that, but I'll have to take the chance," Linden answered. Last night, thinking about this interview, she had wondered if she ought to tell Mrs. Langley about Peter. She knew the confidence would be respected and the explanation accepted. But, although that difficulty was a contributory factor, it was not the main reason for the decision.

"I'll be frank with you, Nurse," Mrs. Langley continued. "As you may know, Nurse Fisher has just got engaged and Nurse Dillon is getting married next month. So far we haven't a replacement for her. As we are already under-staffed your leaving will worsen the position. I don't want to pry into your private life, but are you sure you can't defer your decision for a time?"

"I'm sorry, I wish I could," Linden said uncomfortably. "But it just isn't possible."

Mrs. Langley evidently realised that it was no use persisting. "Very well," she said with a sigh. "There's no more to be said. Naturally you'll have to work out the usual period of notice."

Her usually friendly manner was noticeably cooler

now, and Linden wondered if she had some inkling of the truth and disapproved of flight as an end to the matter.

When Jill heard, she was aghast. "You're crazy, Linden," she exclaimed. "I'm damned if I'd let any man drive me out of a job."

"What makes you think a man has anything to do with it?" Linden asked wearily.

"Well, it *is* that, isn't it?" Jill said, looking wise.

There seemed no point in prevaricating. Linden nodded.

"What are you going to do when you leave here?" her friend asked.

"I don't know yet. Perhaps I can get another job fixed before my notice runs out. I may give up midder altogether."

"Oh, rubbish, you know you love it," Jill said firmly. "I daresay you're right to leave, really. It's pretty hopeless trying to forget about someone who lives in the same town. But there's no point in shelving everything." Although she was plainly curious about what had led to such a drastic step, she tactfully refrained from asking questions.

Another week passed and Linden studied the lists of vacant posts in nursing journals and debated whether to change to private work for a time. She had always wanted to travel, and several advertisements offered attractive jobs in various parts of England and in other countries. She considered leaving England and wrote out a number of applications, but somehow she could not kindle any real enthusiasm. As the days went by, instead of looking to the future, she had a dispiriting sense of time running out, of her whole life foundering on the wreckage of an impossible dream.

She did not tell her parents that she was leaving Melchester. They would be amazed and worried. Her mother was probably busy with the preparations for

Louise's wedding. There was no point in upsetting her as long as it could be postponed.

One afternoon she came home to find an official-looking manila envelope on the doormat. It came from the Colonial Office and invited her to present herself for an interview for a post in Saudi Arabia.

Linden laid the letter on the table and stared at it uncertainly. Then a slight sound from behind her made her glance over her shoulder. Her breath caught in her throat. She had forgotten that the door was still ajar. Coming in laden with parcels, she had left her keys in the latch, dumped her burdens and picked up the letter.

"What are you doing here?" she asked sharply.

Randal shut the door behind him, tossed her keys on to a chair and walked towards her. He ignored the involuntary backward movement she made.

"So you're leaving," he said, his face unreadable.

Linden had forgotten that he would see her letter of resignation at the committee meeting.

"Yes," she said flatly. "I am."

"A rather precipitate step, isn't it?"

She moved to the window. "Is this an official visit?"

He ignored that too. "I want to know why," he said bluntly.

"I don't think it's any of your business." She was only just able to keep her voice steady. How dared he walk in and interrogate her after all that had happened between them!

"Have you got another job?"

Anger bubbled up inside her and boiled over. "As a matter of fact I have," she flared, swinging round. "I'm going to Saudi Arabia. Now if that satisfies your extraordinary curiosity perhaps you wouldn't mind leaving. I'm extremely busy."

She attempted to sweep past him into the kitchen, but he caught her by the shoulder.

"Don't be a fool, Linden," he said abruptly. "You must know why I'm here."

Her heart leapt, but pride made her wrench away. "I neither know nor care," she said frigidly. Then something in his face made her add, "I – I'm sorry I misjudged you about that telephone call. I didn't really believe you could have done it."

"From your attitude earlier that night, I would have thought you considered me capable of anything," he said, his tone hard.

Linden flushed. "I behaved very stupidly," she admitted in a taut voice. Then, as the strain of his nearness became almost unendurable: "Now will you please go!"

"Do you mean that?"

Oh, God, why are you torturing me like this? she thought wildly. Do you want me to admit that I'm in love with you?

"What else could I mean?" she said aloud.

"All right," he said slowly. "If that's really how you want it – I'll go. Perhaps I was wrong all the time."

She heard him cross the room and go out of the door. She wanted to cry out his name, to fling herself into his arms – but she hadn't the courage. Yet if he didn't care for her, why had he come? And what had he meant by 'perhaps I was wrong all the time'? Suddenly she knew that her whole life was balanced on this moment. She could keep her pride and lose all chance of happiness; or she could call him back and chance that her hope was true. Somehow, now that he was walking out of her life, pride didn't seem important any more.

She ran on to the landing and leaned over the banisters. But before she could call to him, there was a shout from the lower flight and a queer thumping sound. Then silence.

Linden flew down the stairs. Randal was lying at

the bottom of the first flight. She could not see his face, but the angle of his body filled her with sudden terror.

"Randal!"

She shot down the lower staircase and bent anxiously over him. He opened his eyes and put a hand up to his head.

"My God! I nearly broke my neck," he said dazedly.

"Don't move. You may have fractured something."

"Don't be silly. I'm just a bit stunned. What the devil did I tread on up there?"

Linden looked round and spotted the cause of his fall. In spite of repeated complaints from the tenants, Jimmy Barnes had left his roller-skates out again.

"That wretched child! He'll kill someone one of these days. Are you sure you're all right?"

Randal shifted himself to lean against the wall behind him. "Yes, I'm fine. Just a ricked ankle."

Instinctively she reached out to feel the ankle, but he caught her hand. "You've been crying," he said.

Linden put a hand up to her cheek. In the anguish of losing him, she had not even known that she was weeping.

"You don't cry over someone you dislike," he said softly. "Why were you crying . . . my love?"

She stared at him unbelievingly. *My love.* Had he really said it?

And then, for the second time, she was held fast in his arms and there was no longer any need for words.

"Well, really!" The exclamation from the doorway made them draw apart.

Jimmy Barnes' grandmother was standing a few feet away, her habitually sour face aghast with outraged propriety.

Linden scrambled to her feet. Strangely, she didn't feel at all discomfited.

"Good afternoon, Mrs. Evans. You'll have to tell Jimmy about his roller-skates," she said politely.

"They were on the stairs again. It really is most dangerous, you know."

Mrs. Evans drew herself up. "Indeed!" she exclaimed. "Well, if you ask me, Nurse Templar, you're in no position to criticise our Jim. Behaving like that in a public place. You're a disgrace to your calling. I've a good mind to report to your superiors!"

"I shouldn't bother, Mrs. Evans." Randal was also on his feet, and he took Linden's hand. "Nurse Templar is leaving here soon. She's just agreed to marry me."

"Oh, has she! Well, that's no excuse for improper goings-on, young man," Mrs. Evans said severely. "I don't know what the world's coming to. Television — that's the trouble today. I've always been against it and I always shall be. They've got no right to show the things they do. It's not decent. Some of them plays aren't fit for people to see."

She stumped up the stairs, muttering angrily.

"Perhaps we had better find somewhere more private," Randal suggested, with a grin.

"Can you manage? Lean on me," Linden offered, as he moved his foot and winced.

"With pleasure." He slipped his arm round her waist and they went upstairs.

In the sitting room, he took her in his arms again. "Do you realise that, but for that kid with the roller-skates, we would probably never have met again?" he asked quietly.

Linden leaned her cheek against his shoulder. "You ought to be resting your ankle," she said dreamily.

"We'll rest it together." He pulled her down on to the couch. "You are going to marry me, aren't you?"

"If you really want me to. I — I still can't believe this is real."

"Any other girl would have known it was real weeks ago," he said, dryly. "What made you so hard to convince?"

"I didn't know you were trying to convince me. You had an awfully strange way of doing it," she protested mildly.

"You didn't make it very easy for me, sweetheart. Most men expect a modicum of encouragement, you know."

"That's the trouble — you aren't like most men," she said wryly. "From the very beginning you seemed to be making a fool of me."

"You'll never quite forgive me for laughing at you on the train, will you?" He was laughing at her now, but with a tenderness in his eyes that made her heart race.

"It wasn't only *on* the train." She explained how she had overheard him describe her to Melanie as a "youthful femme fatale". "I was furious with you."

Randal threw back his head and roared with laughter. "So that was what really cooked my goose," he said, trying to look grave. "Well, it proved to be very apt. You had a fatal effect on me." His amusement faded and he became genuinely serious. "Talking of Melanie, I think perhaps I can tell you the truth about that telephone business now," he said.

"You mean it was Melanie's fault?"

"I'm afraid so. Naturally the chap from the catering firm didn't know any of the guests by name. He took the message and then asked the first person he saw if they could point out Miss Templar to him. That first person happened to be Melanie."

"I see," Linden said slowly. Now that she knew the truth, she wondered why it had not occurred to her before. Melanie must have seen Randal taking her into the garden and, furiously jealous, had seen the message as a means of revenging herself. Perhaps she had hoped that it would result in Linden's dismissal.

"I'm damned if I see," Randal said shortly. "She

187

must have been out of her mind to do such a despicable thing."

"Did you tell her you knew about it?"

"Yes, I told her," he said grimly.

So that accounted for the sudden cruise to Jamaica, Linden thought. But in her new-found happiness, she no longer disliked the other girl. Poor Melanie, she had everything that money could buy and nothing that really mattered.

"Randal," she said suddenly. "I didn't think of it before, but I'm sure Mrs. Craig doesn't like me. She won't approve of this one bit."

"Don't worry, my love. You won't have to live with Adela. I'm going to build that house on the coast that I told you about. That's if you like the idea."

"It sounds heavenly – but what about Andrew and Paula? I'm sure she isn't happy where she is."

"That's settled too. Andrew has finally realised that he can't have it all ways. Adela's been losing her stranglehold on him for some time."

"You mean they're going to have a home of their own? What will your stepmother do?"

"She won't be at a loose end for long. She'll find something or someone to dominate," he said dryly.

"I seem to have misjudged you about that, too," she said regretfully. "I thought you were the one who made life difficult for them all. It would have been very natural for you to dislike Andrew."

"I may well have done as a small boy," he said reflectively. "But the trouble really began after my father's death. Adela was left very well off, but the bulk of the estate – including the company stock – was left to me. Look, do you really want to hear all this now?" He tipped up her chin and lightly kissed her mouth. "Where would you like to go for a honeymoon?" he asked, caressing her cheek.

"Anywhere with you will be heavenly," she said shyly.

His hold tightened and once again she felt the soaring delight that she had experienced before. But this time there was no need to break away.

Eight weeks later, Linden stood on a small wooden balcony above a rocky stream. The grilled blue trout which she had eaten for her supper had been caught in the same stream a few hours earlier. They, and a delicious *quetschen* tart, piled high with rich country cream, were the *specialité de la maison* of this charming little inn lying deep in the Ardennes forests.

The sun was sinking slowly behind the tree-tops as Linden rested her hands on the smooth pinewood balustrade and watched the sky growing dim. Less than twelve hours ago, she and Randal had been married in a London church, Then, after an informal wedding breakfast for their families and a few close friends, they had flown to Brussels and picked up a hired car.

Now, thinking about the day – a day which marked the beginning of a whole new way of life – she found it had been a strange mixture of the most intense happiness and moments of quiet heartache. The most wonderful moment had been when she had walked up the aisle on her father's arm and Randal had turned to smile at her, a look in his eyes that had made her feel like a queen. The saddest moment had been when she had opened a greetings telegram and found that the message wishing her happiness came from Peter Carbury. Dear Peter! She hoped that one day he would find another girl and that she would love him as deeply as he deserved to be loved.

"What are you thinking about, sweetheart?"

She turned. Randal had come into the bedroom without her hearing him. He was leaning against the doorway, smiling at her.

"I was wondering if I deserve to have all this," she said softly.

He came to stand beside her, his arms round her waist. "I know I don't deserve anyone as lovely as you, sweet." His lips brushed her temple.

She leaned her head against his shoulder. "I have so much," she said dreamily. "A fortnight with you in these heavenly woods, and furnishing our house by the sea and having babies and ... oh, everything a woman could want." She lifted her head and looked up at him. "The innkeeper's daughter is pregnant, did you notice? I spoke to her on my way up and she said the baby is due at any moment."

Randal laughed. "You've retired – remember?" he said, teasingly. "If you're thinking of lending a hand, you'd better forget it. For the next two weeks I want you all to myself."

"So you've started browbeating me already. I was afraid you would." She freed herself from his arm and went back into the bedroom. The summer was almost over, and now that the sun had set, there was a hint of September in the air.

Randal closed the balcony doors and came to stand behind her as she brushed her hair. She looked at his reflection in the mirror, and it was wonderful to be free of all the wretchedness and doubt which had once tormented her.

She put the brush back on the dressing table and the soft glow of the oil lamp lit a crimson fire in the ruby on her third finger. But beautiful as the engagement ring was, it was the slim platinum band below it which was most precious to her. The ruby was a symbol of their hopes, but the wedding ring set the seal on their future together.